When Francie heard a knock at the door, she flew off the sofa and stood hyperventilating in the middle of the small room. She calmed herself down by repeating, "The fruit of the spirit is love, joy, peace, patience…" as she moved toward the door and opened it.

There Mr. Fairchild stood, all six feet plus of him, dressed in a light blue shirt, blue patterned tie and blue slacks. No jacket today—probably wise, with the heat.

At the moment she knew why it had been so important for her to clean up the apartment, why she hadn't wanted him to see the dump in the first place and why making a good impression on him was so important to her.

The reason was simple: she didn't think of him as only her parole officer. She saw him as an attractive man. Of course, any woman would see Brandon Fairchild as an incredibly handsome man. Obviously she was no exception.

JANE MYERS PERRINE

grew up in Kansas City, Missouri, has a B.A. from Kansas State University and has an M.Ed. in Spanish from the University of Louisville. She has taught high school Spanish in five states. Presently she teaches in the beautiful hill country of Texas. Her husband is minister of a Christian church in central Texas where Jane teaches an adult Sunday school class. Jane was a finalist in the Regency category of the Golden Heart. Her short pieces have appeared in the *Houston Chronicle, Woman's World* magazine and other publications. The Perrines share their home with two spoiled cats and an arthritic cocker spaniel. Readers can visit her Web page at www.janemyersperrine.com.

THE PATH
TO LOVE

JANE MYERS PERRINE

Steeple
Hill®

Published by Steeple Hill Books™

STEEPLE HILL BOOKS

Steeple
Hill®

ISBN 0-373-81224-8

THE PATH TO LOVE

www.SteepleHill.com

Printed in U.S.A.

The fruit of the Spirit is love, joy,
peace, patience, kindness, generosity,
faithfulness, gentleness and self-control.
—*Galatians* 5:22-23

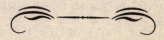

This book is dedicated to Jeannie Gray.
A dear friend, a wonderful writer and a
joyful spirit. We miss you very much.

And to my dear husband, George,
who has generously shared his faith and love
with me for so many years.

Chapter One

Francie Calhoun learned to pick pockets when she was five, mark cards at eight and hotwire a car years before she could get a driver's license.

At the age of sixteen, with all the adults in her family living at the expense of the great state of Texas, Francie was pretty much alone.

Life hadn't improved a whole lot since then. Eight years had passed, eighteen months of which she'd spent in prison. She could see no hope until after a twelve-hour shift waiting tables she stopped in front of a church for absolutely no reason except she was so tired she couldn't take another step.

She had hesitated outside the church, but was finally drawn inside against her will. She stepped through the wide doors and looked around the sanctuary. The entire audience was standing and smiling, their voices joyfully joined in a hymn—something about saving a wretch like me.

The words fell upon her like spring rain, soothing her nerves and refreshing her soul. She slipped down a side aisle and found a place on the end of a bench.

"Here's where we are," the woman next to her said with a smile as she handed Francie a book and pointed at the verse of the song they were singing.

"Thank you." Francie nodded at the woman.

As she sang uncertainly, trying to fit the words with the unfamiliar music, Francie could feel pain and anger rolling out of her.

For the next thirty minutes she joined the singing and prayed, hands clasped in front of her and eyes closed just as she saw the lady do.

Then the Reverend Mr. Jonah Miles stepped to the front of the platform. He wasn't an impressive figure: thin and bald, wearing a white suit that seemed too big for him. But when he began to speak, his deep, assured voice wound a spell around the audience. He seemed to grow taller.

He spoke of love and redemption, mercy

and grace. It wasn't at all like the hell-fire-and-damnation stuff her mother had taken Francie to with the hope her daughter would be a good girl if the preacher could fill her with fear. *That* had failed terribly.

But the message of the Reverend Mr. Miles entered Francie's heart and healed it, filling in deep cracks and crevices left by a hard and lonely life, a troubled existence.

"Here, child." The nice woman handed Francie a tissue. It was only then she realized tears were streaming down her cheeks.

Almost an hour after he'd begun to preach, the Reverend Mr. Miles asked anyone who had been saved to come forward. Francie thought she might have been but wasn't sure enough to join the crowd headed toward the front.

After the last hymn was sung, she left, filled with such wonder and buoyancy that she knew she'd be there the next evening.

But, when she went back, the church was dark and empty and the Reverend Mr. Miles was gone.

When she met Brandon Fairchild, her new parole officer, the next week, he was skeptical of Francie's conversion.

"Miss Calhoun, I don't believe for a minute that you've changed." Mr. Fairchild looked up from the file he held in front of him. "As I look through your life of crime, I see a history of con games and manipulating the truth, as well as that robbery conviction. A lot of deception, three convictions and not a word of remorse."

"I am sorry for everything I did, Mr. Fairchild. I truly am," she said to his frowning countenance.

He closed the folder, took off his reading glasses, and stared at Francie with eyes as cold as the metal furnishings of his small, gray cubicle. "Is that all you have to say?"

At the moment, she couldn't think of anything more. Odd, because usually she was never at a loss for words. Attempting to explain what had happened to her the other night to this disapproving man seemed impossible. Francie looked down at her hands and took a deep breath before returning her gaze to her parole officer.

He certainly was handsome. Rumpled blond hair and a face that would have made her artistic aunt Tessie long to paint it. Unfortunately, Aunt Tessie was serving eight to ten for forgery and fraud.

His white shirt displayed broad shoulders, while the loosened tie and open collar button showed a muscular neck. About thirty, he was good-looking enough to tempt a woman to do what she shouldn't, and pretty enough to make every sensible word—and a lot of foolish ones—flee Francie's brain.

In spite of that gorgeous exterior, he was cold. His hard gray glare froze her to the bone. She'd never convince him she was telling the truth.

Again, her smart mouth deserted her. Francie swallowed before she mumbled, "I went to church last Friday."

"And?"

"And it changed me." That was good. She sat up and met his eyes. "I'm going to try to be a better person." She shook her head. "No, I'm going to *be* a better person."

He leafed through a few pages of the folder. "I see you were redeemed once before, four years ago."

"That wasn't real. That was a con. Besides, I was never charged with anything that time." Her appearance and sincerity had always been her ace in the hole. Thin, with curly black hair, innocent blue eyes and freckles, she looked young and guileless and could almost always talk her mark out of pressing charges. Too bad she wasn't having any luck convincing Mr. Fairchild.

"So *that* conversion was a con? Would you explain the difference this time?"

"This isn't a con." She leaned forward and gave him the sincere look she'd perfected after years of practice. "You have to understand. This is real."

He smiled but there was no humor in his expression. "Oh, I see. *This* one is real."

"Please believe me. I had a real experience that healed me, inside." She pressed her hands on her chest.

But he shook his head.

"It happened," she said. "I know it's hard to believe. I mean, you have my record right there in front of you, so you know I haven't always been honest, but please, don't doubt what happened. Don't put it down because of my past. This one was real. Really."

For a few seconds, he stopped smiling and studied her seriously before he laughed. "You *are* good. I read that in your file." He looked at the tab on the folder. "Let's see. Mr. Gentry, your last parole officer, wrote, 'Frances Margaret Calhoun can make anyone believe anything.' That's right." He shook his head. "You almost had me there."

Francie sat back in her chair with a sigh. "But it *is* true." Goodness, she couldn't remember the last time she'd failed to convince someone about something.

"Okay, so if you're redeemed, if you've truly gone through a religious transformation, where did you go to church Sunday?"

"I didn't go." That was a mistake, both for her sake and for a chance to convince Mr. Fairchild. She should have gone back Sunday morning instead of studying for a test.

He lifted his eyebrow. "I think going to church would be the first thing you would do."

"Well, you're right. I'm just not in the habit of that yet. Besides, not all churches welcome ex-cons."

"The right one will. If you are sincere, the only way you'll know is by giving the churches a try."

She nodded.

"All right, Miss Calhoun. Why don't you tell me how else you have changed your life?"

"I don't know yet," she confessed. "I mean, it just happened. I'm kind of new at this. I don't know exactly where to start."

"Miss Calhoun, I sincerely hope you've

changed, but you're going to have to convince me. That's not going to be easy. You're going to have to stay clean."

"I'm going to stay clean and not only because I want to convince you."

He shuffled through the papers and notes in her record again. "I notice Gentry didn't keep up on your hours at work." He looked at another page. "Are you still a waitress at the Best Diner?"

She nodded. Her former parole officer hadn't kept track of much of anything in the months before he retired.

"You need to bring me your pay stubs so I can verify employment."

She nodded again.

"How many hours a week are you working?"

"As many as I can get. Thirty-five to fifty."

"And you still live in an apartment on Dixon Street?"

Hardly an apartment. "Yes."

He made a note and checked a form. "All right. Bring me that pay stub. Keep out of trouble if you want to convince me. And work on those changes in your life." He looked up at her frigidly for a second before closing her file and picking up another.

"That's the problem," she confided. "I still don't know how to even begin with this religion thing. I mean, I'm going to find a church, but what do I do next?"

He thought for a moment. "If you want a place to start, you might try the fruit of the spirit."

"You mean, like grapes?"

This time his smile was genuine but lasted barely a second and hardly warmed his eyes. "If you're sincere, you'll find that out for yourself." He opened the other folder. "I'll see you in two weeks."

"When Mr. Gentry was my parole officer, I only came once a month."

"I work differently." He frowned at her. "I want to see you in two weeks to make sure you're headed in the right direction." He wrote a few words on his appointment calendar. "And I am going to have to visit your work site and your apartment in the next few weeks. I see Gentry didn't do that, either."

"No, he didn't."

"I think that's everything we have time for today." He stood and held out his hand. "Good-bye, Miss Calhoun."

Francie took it. He had nice, strong hands, even some calluses on them, as if he'd worked in the yard or something. She turned to leave.

"Oh, Miss Calhoun, don't forget church on Sunday."

She looked back. "Isn't that against the law? Mentioning religion?"

"Not if you've chosen it to be part of your rehabilitation program. However, I will expand my statement. I suggest you attend the temple, synagogue, mosque, church, cathedral or other religious establishment of your choice."

"Thank you." She left the office feeling a little off balance.

Before his retirement a month earlier, Mr. Gentry had only barked out a few questions having to do with her recent incarceration for holding up a convenience store and asked how work was going, then dismissed her with a wave of his hand. Mr. Fairchild seemed both more interested and more judgmental, almost as though he didn't like her. He certainly didn't trust her. Not that that was a bad thing. She wouldn't trust an ex-con, either.

She wasn't sure if she liked Mr. Fairchild's approach or not. What she *did* know was that she was stuck with him.

* * *

The next day at work, Francie asked her boss Julie Sullivan, the owner of the diner, and her regular customers if they'd heard of the fruit of the spirit. One suggestion sounded good.

Julie said maybe apples or cherries because a nice slice of pie always lifted her spirit. But, in the end, the consensus was, well, no one had the slightest idea.

"The fruit of the spirit," Francie repeated as she walked up and down the aisles at a religious bookstore the next afternoon.

Unable to find anything in the sections loaded with CDs, books on the end of time and T-shirts covered with bright pictures and Bible verses—at least, she guessed that's what the phrases must be—Francie finally went to the checkout counter and asked, "Where would I find something about the fruit of the spirit?"

An older woman with tightly permed hair and owlish glasses said, "Romans," without even looking up. Then she shouted over her shoulder. "Isn't that right, Harvey? Fruit of the spirit—isn't that in Romans?"

"She might want to look at Galatians five," said the white-haired man. "Nice list there.

Can't remember the verses." He smiled at Francie and turned back to some papers he'd been checking.

"Okay, try Galatians five." The woman picked up a pencil and started marking off items.

Well, what the—Francie's thoughts started until she reminded herself to start watching her language. What did all that Romans and Galatians stuff mean? But all she could see was the top of the woman's tight curls and the back of the white-haired man's head. They looked so busy she hated to bother them again. Instead she returned to wandering around the store, feeling incredibly dumb.

"Are you looking for something?" a high-school girl asked the third time Francie passed her.

"I need to learn about the fruit of the spirit. Something about Romans and Galatians, I think."

"Why don't you look it up in your Bible?"

Ah, so that's where Romans and Galatians could be found. Why hadn't Francie thought of that? She looked around. "Where would I find a Bible?"

"You're new at this, aren't you?" The girl smiled. "I'll show you."

Within seconds they were in an area Francie'd passed through before. The girl waved her arm at an entire case of books. "Here are the Bibles."

"Those are *all* Bibles?" Francie studied the six-foot-high shelves that stretched forever across the room. The books were of all different colors, from black to white with shades of red and brilliant blue and somber brown. Some faced forward to show pictures or symbols. There were hardbacks and others with paper or leather or plastic covers. She shook her head. This was getting a lot harder and more complicated than she'd thought it would be.

"What are you looking for?"

"I don't know. Just a regular Bible. How do I know which one?" The silver Bible with a hologram on the front looked interesting but not very…well…religious. Then she noticed the prices. "Are the more expensive Bibles better? I mean, do they have more words and stories in them?" She tried to remember how much money she had—a couple of dollar bills, a five, some quarters. Yeah, price was important.

The young woman smiled again. "No, the only difference is the translation and the binding. Find one that you like to read. You can find something cheap. It'll have the same thing the more expensive ones have."

The task still seemed overwhelming. "Which one do you like?"

"This one's good." She took one from a shelf and handed it to Francie, then added several more, helping Francie look at the different versions.

After she read a few lines in each, Francie found one she liked and could afford. "Thank you," she said.

The young woman took Francie's hand and said, "It was a blessing to meet you."

What do you know? It was a blessing to meet her. A lovely thought. "It was a blessing to meet you, too."

Francie paid, then hurried back to her apartment, grasping the bag with the Bible inside tightly.

Not much of an apartment, she reflected as she closed the door. Not even an efficiency. Once up the three flights of stairs and inside, she could take five strides and be at the only window—which overlooked the alley. On the right was a sofa bed; to the left in a tiny kitchen was a card table covered with a bright-yellow checked tablecloth.

Around the walls were splashes of brilliance: Aunt Tessie's forged impressionistic paintings, fifteen that Francie had saved from the police and would guard until her aunt's return. They were beautiful and brought so much color into the small room that Francie didn't need light or a view from the window. Besides, with the pictures in place, only inches of the flaking green walls showed.

She settled on the threadbare sofa and opened the book.

It wasn't all that hard to find Galatians. In the front, she found an index and turned to the right page. Once there, she discovered that some thoughtful person had divided the book using numbers in large, bold print. In no time, she found Galatians five. Scanning the chapter, she read to herself the words: "'…the fruit of the Spirit is love, joy, peace, patience, kindness, generosity, faithfulness, gentleness and self-control.'"

Francie ran her finger across the words as she read them again. Finally, she whispered to herself as she read, "'love, joy, peace, patience, kindness, generosity, faithfulness, gentleness and self-control.'" With a nod, she added, "I like that."

She closed the Bible and looked at how

thick it was. Then she looked at the end of the last book—1,402 pages. She hadn't read that much in her entire life. The thought of finishing that many pages overwhelmed her.

Francie sat back in the chair and sighed. Why had she thought she could do this? People like white-haired Harvey and the clerk in book store had probably been reading the Bible since they were kids. Even the young woman who'd been so helpful had probably spent more years reading the Bible than Francie had wasted being a troublemaker in school.

And Mr. Fairchild must have read lots and lots of it. He knew about the fruit of the spirit.

How could she even attempt this? But, if she wanted to change, Francie knew she had to tackle all these pages. Francie Calhoun was not a quitter.

Where should she begin? Obviously at the beginning. It would take her an eternity to finish all of it but she had to, really had to.

Besides, the Reverend Mr. Jonah Miles and that nice lady at the church had probably read the entire book. They'd started her on this road. She couldn't let them down. She was behind, but that didn't mean she shouldn't try.

She said to herself, "'…love, joy, peace, patience, kindness, generosity, faithfulness, gentleness, and self-control….' That is a good place to start."

Chapter Two

Too impatient to wait for the elevator, Francie reminded herself that she *had* to work on this problem of constantly running behind as she dashed up three flights of stairs in the Austin, Texas, courthouse annex. She glanced at the clock on the landing—ten minutes after ten. She was only a few minutes late, but she was also panting and her hair was a springy mess. On top of that, her cheeks must be bright red from the exertion of running from the bus stop.

Terrific, she mumbled. Here she'd wanted to impress Mr. Fairchild with what a fine citizen she was, and she couldn't even arrive on time for her second appointment. She stopped just inside the door of the parole office and attempted to slow her breathing.

From the cubicles, separated from each other with six-foot-high gray metal walls, she could hear the low buzz of voices. Telephones rang from the offices that surrounded the cubicles. Parolees waited on hard wooden benches, reading or sleeping, while others wandered through the open space drinking coffee and talking.

In spite of the chaos in the small area, she was aware of Mr. Fairchild who sat quietly and alone in his cubicle scanning a page of a file folder.

Oh, my, he was absolutely gorgeous. When she saw him, she wished she was at least three or four inches taller and a few pounds heavier. And wouldn't she love to have something to wear besides jeans and ratty tennis shoes? And, while she was wishing, wouldn't it be nice to be absolutely gorgeous, too?

With a pat to the top of her head, she attempted to tame her wild curls as she walked across the scuffed gray vinyl floor toward his desk. "Mr. Fairchild?"

He glanced up, saw her, stood and reached his hand out toward her. She took it and smiled. He had such a nice, strong grip.

"Miss Calhoun." He nodded. "I was looking over your file and realize Gentry didn't keep up with you very well."

"No, he didn't. I was assigned to Mr. Gentry when I got out of prison six months ago. I think he was winding down for retirement."

"That may be true. Nevertheless, I still need some very basic information about you. There's almost nothing written here other than the dates of your appointments and your address."

As he read further, he tapped his pen, silver with what looked like his initials engraved on the side. "I find no mention of what you discussed during your appointments. He didn't keep up with your employment or much of anything else, no information from your trial or prison records." He looked up at Francie. "That's not at all professional."

Professional must be very important to him, Francie thought as she put her book on the floor and leaned forward. "I think he was really burned out."

"It's kind of you to say that, but I can't be as forgiving."

Wow! He thought she was both kind *and* forgiving. That was at least one fruit of the spirit. "Thank you."

"Miss Calhoun, *you* shouldn't be forgiving, either, not in this case. A parole officer is supposed to assist you to return to the community as an honest, upright citizen. Gentry let you down."

She nodded. He was right.

"Let me check on the information I have." He read a few lines. "Your father, aunt and uncle are all—"

"Incarcerated."

"Your mother?"

"I don't know where she is. She walked out on us when my father was arrested. I was six."

"Who brought you up?"

"Oh, different people, off and on. Usually, when they weren't incarcerated, my uncle Lou and aunt Tessie, my father's brother and sister. Larceny runs in my family, I fear."

"You believe it is a genetic characteristic?"

"Yes," she said with a sigh. "I'm afraid so, but I'm working hard and hoping to overcome that unfortunate trait."

"Commendable, Miss Calhoun."

He glanced at his watch, a lovely thin silver-colored one. Expensive, she thought. Of course she knew nothing about watches. Maybe it wasn't as costly as it looked.

"Oh, it's probably getting close to time for your next appointment. I'm sorry I was late." She put a hand against her cheek. It felt warm. "I had a test that lasted much longer than I thought it would. The bus was late so I had to run all the way from the bus stop. I thought I'd be here sooner but I kept dropping stuff and the lights held me up." She took a deep breath. "I'm sorry. I do hate to keep people waiting."

"A test?" he asked. "Are you not feeling well? I don't believe I've read anything here about health problems." He leafed through the pages to check.

"No, not a medical test. English lit. Jane Austen. You know, she writes wonderful characters and she's really funny, not what I'd expected from the classics." She scooted forward on the chair and whispered, "Have you ever read *Pride and Prejudice?*"

"Yes I have…but why did you take a test on *Pride and Prejudice?* Why are you even reading it? I remember being forced to read parts of it in high school. I also remember it was slow and not very interesting."

"Oh, no, it's wonderful." She sat back and pondered for a moment. "Even though they lived in a totally different time, those people are incredibly interesting. They're not all that much different from us."

"You're reading Jane Austen for pleasure?"

"No, no, for English lit, but if I'd known it was so much fun, I'd have read it years ago."

"Miss Calhoun," he shook his head. "I'm afraid I don't understand. Would you please explain why you are reading *Pride and Prejudice*."

"Isn't it in my file?" She moved forward and tried to read the record upside down. "Didn't Mr. Gentry mention that I'm working on an associate's degree, picking up the required courses?"

He frowned at her information sheet. "How can you do that? Gentry's notes say you don't have a high-school diploma."

"What do you mean?" She tried to read her file again, again unsuccessfully. "It's not in there, is it? I got my GED while I was incarcerated."

He looked up at her, his eyebrow lifted. "You did? Congratulations. I'll get that information from TDC and put it in your record." He wrote on a sticky note and attached it to her folder. "Did you bring me your pay stubs?"

She put her hand over her mouth. "Oh, no! I had them all ready to go, then I got worried because I had forgotten if Elizabeth Bennett had—well, you probably don't care about what I had to check, but I thought it might be on the test. Anyway, I left them on the table when I ran out. Can I...may I bring them next time?"

"Of course." He studied her for a moment before he asked. "How is the great metamorphosis going? I mean, have you moved along with your change?"

"Yes, my *metamorphosis* is moving along just fine." She studied him for a moment before she nodded and said, "I *do* know what the word means."

"Of course you do. I had no doubt—"

"You know, *criminal* doesn't mean stupid, except on certain topics, like hard work and honesty and common sense. Truly, I'm working hard not to fall into that trap again. Self-control is high on the list of fruit of the spirit, one I'm concentrating very hard on."

"Of course, Miss Calhoun. Please forgive my rudeness. I have to say that I'm very pleased you have found out what the fruit of the spirit is."

"Thank you." She felt surprisingly delighted at the compliment. "Okay. About the metamorphosis, I'm still looking for a church." She held her hand up before he could ask. "The Sunday after I saw you, I went to the first one I visited, the one where I decided I wanted to change. The people there didn't seem happy to see me. Guess they don't mind if I come to the revival service but not Sunday morning." She shrugged. "That evening, I visited another church, but it was a little, well, a little *too* loud for me. Last Sunday, I tried another but that was… ummm…slightly boring and the people seemed a little cold. So I'm still looking for one that will be right."

"If you're sincere, I'm sure you'll find a place." He picked up his pen again. "Why don't you tell me about your plans for the future? Why did you decide to go to college?" He wrote the date and looked up expectantly.

She didn't speak for almost a minute. She bit her lower lip before saying, "I don't know what I'm going to do with that education," she said finally. "I just knew, when I went to prison, that I couldn't live like that anymore, like I always had, like my family always has. Stealing from people and hiding from the police and being locked up. I knew I had to prepare for a better life."

He nodded his encouragement.

"My family hasn't been much for looking ahead. I mean, past the next job or casing the convenience store or bank they wanted to knock over or setting up their next scam. Planning is new for me, too, but I have to change. I know education is the place to start."

She looked at him for a second, then she gave him a tiny, uncertain smile which grew into a grin.

His expression changed from concentration to—it looked like interest. Oh, she knew she had to be wrong, but maybe a spark of attraction was there, for just a second. Then he blinked, cleared his throat and assumed an unsmiling professional demeanor.

"Education seems like, for my mind, what those fruit of the spirit are for my soul, you know?" she continued. "I'd like to use my education to help people, to become a teacher, maybe."

He didn't say anything for a minute, just kept his eyes on her face until he realized she was watching him while he studied her. "I'm sorry, Miss Calhoun. An idea about another client distracted me. If you would please repeat your comment?"

It didn't seem to her he'd been thinking about another client. He'd been looking at her, sort of inspecting her face, as if he found her attractive. She wasn't going to call him on it. How dumb would it be to contradict her parole officer? How dumb was it to think he could find Francie Calhoun attractive?

Instead she said, "I said I thought once about maybe being a teacher, although I don't think a school would hire anyone with my record."

"That's probably right." He used a cold, professional tone.

She shivered at the unexpected chill in his words. Why had he changed so much? And he seemed to be meditating again, looking down as his pen before pulling his attention back to her.

"I'm sorry," he said. "There's an enormous problem with the other client. Please continue, Miss Calhoun." He didn't meet her eyes.

"How nice of you to be so concerned about all your clients. I don't think Mr. Gentry thought about us at all."

"Nevertheless, I should not be taking time from your appointment."

"I figure nursing is out, too, and probably accounting, so I don't know what I want to do, what's open to me. I'm just picking up the basic hours."

"I'll arrange for you to see a vocational counselor." He wrote another note on her file.

"Thank you." She blinked in surprise at his suggestion. Mr. Gentry would never have thought of that. "That's a wonderful idea. They could give me some direction."

"I appreciate your gratitude, but it's nothing. Gentry should have done this months ago."

"It's something I could certainly use."

"Miss Calhoun," he began but his voice seemed to go all funny, alternating between friendly interest and that chilling note. She wondered why. If she hadn't known better, she'd think maybe he *did* find her attractive and was trying to ignore it, but that was crazy. She was, she reminded herself, an ex-con. He was, after all, her parole officer.

Did he have to keep reminding himself, too? She wondered for a moment before stuffing that thought back in the far depths of her brain. Of course not. He was her parole officer and would never find a woman with her criminal tendencies interesting.

"Miss Calhoun," he said after clearing his throat, "how many hours do you have in college?"

"Oh, only fifteen so far. Nine when I was incarcerated and six since—but I'll have twenty-one when I get my credit for this course and the intro to psych course I'm taking. I wish it could go faster but it's hard to work and go to school. I work breakfast, from five-thirty to nine or so, and lunch. Julie lets me work in a morning class between nine and ten when I need to, and in the fall, I'll take two in the afternoon. And, of course, the cost—"

"Have you checked into scholarship help or grants?"

"What?" She considered for a moment. "No, I haven't. Would I be eligible? I didn't think people like me—"

"There are some government funds that are closed to anyone with a record, but I believe there are others you could apply for. I'll write a note to get in touch with your school. What school are you attending?"

"Texas Community College, the downtown branch."

He nodded again. "I know someone in the financial aid office. I'll give her a call."

"You are the nicest man." She leaned forward and placed her hand on his.

He quickly moved his hand to pick up his coffee cup. She probably shouldn't have touched him.

"I'm sorry." Embarrassed, she sat back in her chair. "It's just that no one has ever made an effort to help me like this. Thank you."

"Gentry should have." The chill clung to his voice. "I guess that's all, Miss Calhoun."

Brandon kept his eyes on his pen. Not that there was anything interesting in the silver tube, but he refused to look at Miss Calhoun's face. Her blue eyes probably showed confusion and hurt over his attempts at aloofness and his hot-and-cold behavior. That couldn't concern him at this moment. The point was to be professional because right now he didn't feel at all professional. Not a bit.

He was attracted to her probably because he didn't meet all that many women in this job. After a second, he had to admit that was not an acceptable explanation. It wasn't an explanation at all.

Then he had to remind himself he was not interested in Miss Calhoun. He could not possibly be attracted to a felon. He was only interested in her as a man would be interested in any pretty young woman.

He could not possibly be attracted to Miss Calhoun. She was medium height and thin. With all that curly black hair, she wasn't really pretty. The freckles dotted across her fair skin made her cute, but not pretty. He'd never been drawn to cute women.

But there was such a sparkle about her. She was so full of life and joy. Hope glowed in her eyes. Why would a woman with such a background feel optimistic about her life?

There certainly was little future in a relationship between the two of them. After all, Miss Calhoun was certainly not the type of woman he could bring home to meet his mother.

Where in the world had that idea come from? He jerked his attention back to his client and looked at the calendar. "Two weeks, Miss Calhoun? Same time?"

"Perhaps a few minutes later, ten-thirty? My class is from nine to nine-fifty. If I can catch the bus right away ten o'clock is usually fine, but today it was hard to get here on time because—"

He cut her off before she could complete the sentence and shooed her away with his hand. "Ten-thirty is fine." He jotted a note in her file and slid it into the cabinet. He needed businesslike gestures to remind himself who she was and who *he* was.

But he couldn't keep himself from watching her walk away from his desk. When she got to the door, she turned. Her eyes met his and she smiled unevenly at him.

Callously, he dropped his glance to his desk, but he could not wipe out the memory of her face and the charm of her smile, so genuine and full of delight and interest, as if she cared about him and his reaction, as if she hoped he shared her happiness.

Mixed with that picture was the memory of her uncooperative black curls and those wide and oddly innocent eyes that could also sparkle with humor or pain, the hurt she tried so carefully to hide. In their depths, he glimpsed anger which she also tried to disguise, attempting to make a good impression on him, he guessed. What she didn't realize was that she already had. Too good an impression. He was even starting to believe her. Not wise to believe a parolee.

Other than her incredible smile—which he was sure she'd used to con countless others—and many physical attributes, why did he care about Miss Calhoun? She was no different from the other ex-cons he worked with, not a bit.

Not a single bit, he repeated to himself. He didn't know yet, but he guessed she was as untruthful and manipulative as many of them. Then, why was he so concerned about this one, about her?

This was not at all the emotion he should be experiencing when talking to a parolee. Being interested in a client, he lectured himself, was incredibly unprofessional. If he acted on it, if she even guessed he was attracted to her, he could get in a great deal of legal trouble. In addition, he didn't want to make Miss Calhoun uncomfortable, didn't want her to think he was harassing her in any way. She needed to believe his interest in her was completely professional.

Oh, he always helped the parolees he worked with. There was nothing new about that. He'd always thought that was his duty as a Christian. He helped them find work, financial aid, housing, even food, but never with the need, almost a compulsion, he felt to help Miss Calhoun.

But there was something odd about her, something that nagged him. He flipped the folder open and scanned her record. Several arrests, two convictions on scams but no time served. Then this robbery. Strange she would turn from being a con artist to a robber. It happened, of course, people changed, but she didn't look like a violent person.

He slammed the folder shut. What did he know? She was a convicted felon and his client, only that.

Then he looked up into the scarred, beefy face of Butch Conway who stood in front of his desk. Butch had returned to society after a ten-year stay in Huntsville for assault with time off for good behavior.

All thoughts of the attractive-but-felonious Francie Calhoun fled to the back of his brain as he began his work to mold Butch into a model citizen.

"So, how's this hunk of a parole officer of yours?" Julie Sullivan, owner of the diner, put two cups of coffee and a slice of apple pie on the table and joined Francie in the booth where she was reading for her English lit class.

Francie looked up at Julie and shook her head, attempting to return from Shakespeare's flower-scented bower in the Forest of Avon to the smell of bacon and syrup left over from breakfast in Julie's tiny diner.

It was a nice, neat little place with a black-and-white checkerboard floor. The table tops were beige with chairs and booths upholstered in red. The windows looking out on the busy street were covered with beige curtains with red piping. Against the walls were six booths— empty now except for Francie and Julie—with eight square tables in the open space.

"Oh, I don't know. I mean, I hate to call him a hunk when our relationship is purely professional."

"You called him that before and didn't seem to mind." Julie poured two packets of creamer into her cup and stirred, keeping her eyes on Francie's face as she pushed a strand of her graying black curls back in place, curls Francie had noticed barely ever moved on their own.

"Two weeks ago, he didn't feel so...I don't know. He got a little stuffy at the last appointment, sort of cold. Oh, not that he wasn't helpful," she hurried to add. "He seemed different this time, not as friendly."

"That's not unusual. You know how men are. I mean, Manny can be a real jerk sometimes, when he's feeling real macho."

"I don't know. That might be it." Francie shrugged and looked back at her book. "Sorry, Julie, but I have to read the rest of this play."

"I won't bother you for long. We've got a good two hours before the lunch crowd comes in. You might as well take a break." She pushed the cup and the pie in front of Francie. "This is your boss talking. Do what I say. You're getting too thin. Eat."

"Yes, ma'am." The coffee was strong and

hot, and the pie tasted wonderful, warm and cinnamon-flavored. "Okay, Julie, suppose you tell me what's going on with you and Manny while we're taking this break together."

"Nothing's going on between us. You should know that. Since I broke our engagement last year, we've never looked back. He dates other women; I date men, lots of men." She looked over her shoulder at the dark, handsome cook.

"He's just like all men," Julie continued.

"I think he's more handsome than most, Julie."

She bit her lip. "Yes, I guess he is. He's got those dark brown eyes that say such romantic things to a woman, but he's got a really macho attitude. Thinks he owns his woman and can't get it through his head that I have a brain and can take care of myself. He hates it that I own this place." She leaned toward Francie. "I think the fact that I was his boss and told him I would not hand the diner over to him when we got married was what finally broke us up." She sat back in the booth. "Men!"

"You know, it's probably hard for him to work for the woman he loves."

"What?" Julie sat up straighter. "What's the matter with you? You used to agree with me about Manny."

"I'm trying that kindness thing."

"Huh?"

"I'm trying to be a kinder person."

"Just because you're trying to change doesn't mean you have to side with Manny. You're still my friend and can be kind to *me*."

"I'm trying not to judge other people."

"If that doesn't beat all." She took a sip of her coffee. "I want you to be happy, Francie, but don't get all goody-goody on me."

"I'm sorry, Julie. Sometimes it's hard to know exactly the right balance. I'm still searching."

"I guess you're doing the best you can." Julie stood. "Okay, I'll leave you to your play." Julie picked up the coffee cups and took them to the kitchen.

When Francie was alone, she leaned against the back of the bench and closed her eyes, turning her thoughts toward God. *"You know,"* she whispered, *"this whole transformation is turning out to be a lot more difficult than I ever imagined. I'd appreciate a little help here because I don't know what I'm doing."*

Francie had just finished studying when the lunch crowd came in. Within minutes, she had tables and booths full and was running back and forth, taking orders and picking them up, placing them on tables, adding up checks and picking up tips. While she did all of this, she smiled and kept up running jokes with the regulars.

Shortly before one-thirty, the crowd thinned. As she filled the glasses of the few remaining customers and wiped down tables, she heard a familiar voice.

"Hey, Curly, how're you doing?"

Francie turned around to see her cousin Mike Fuller, Tessie's older son. "Hi there. How's one of my favorite cousins doing?"

He had become such a handsome young man. She'd met him when he was seven and she was twelve, back when Uncle Lou went to prison and she'd moved in with Aunt Tessie. For six years, they'd been like sister and brother. He'd been a skinny little kid, a runt everyone in the neighborhood picked on. Now he was over six feet tall, broad from working out and almost as handsome as Mr. Fairchild.

Where had that foolish thought come from? Mike was much more handsome than Mr. Fairchild, in a different sort of way. Besides, she shouldn't be thinking of her parole officer like that. She shouldn't be thinking of him at all.

"Hey, Francie." He hugged her.

"Sit down. What do you want? The usual?"

"Yeah. You know how much I love Manny's hamburgers."

"Hi, kid," Julie said and gave Mike a hug. "Take a break, Francie, and grab a bite with Mike." She picked up the order Francie had written and handed it to Manny who took it from Julie's hand but didn't look at her.

"Friendly guy," Julie grumbled.

"Hey, Mike," shouted Manny from the window. Then he turned toward Julie to say, "See, I'm a very friendly guy when people treat me right."

Julie frowned. "If you weren't such a good cook and never missed a day of work, I'd fire you." She picked up a plate and carried it to a customer.

"What a terrific surprise," Francie said to Mike. "What are you doing here? Don't you have class?" She slid into the booth next to him.

"Hey, lay off. I don't have classes this afternoon, and I'm not due at work for an hour. Why can't I stop by to see my favorite cousin—"

"Only cousin."

"Without getting the third degree?"

"The third degree is sort of a custom with our family." She smiled at him. "How's life going?"

"Great. My grades are good. You know I got accepted to med school."

"I know. I don't think I've ever been happier."

Mike took her hand. "If it hadn't been for you—" He shook his head. "Thanks, Francie."

"Enough of that." She shook her head. "Okay, so tell me why you're here."

"My girlfriend's family is having a barbecue Sunday. She's heard me talk about you and wants you to come." He put onions and ketchup on the hamburger Julie had just placed in front of him, then took a drink of the milkshake. "We're going to start about noon."

"That sounds wonderful, but I'll probably be a little late." She paused and dropped her eyes to the plate Julie had placed in front of her. "I...um...I'm going to church on Sunday."

If he hadn't had taken a big bite of hamburger, Francie knew Mike's mouth would have fallen open. While he chewed and swallowed, she picked up the tuna salad sandwich Julie had given her and nibbled on a corner.

"You're going to church? Why? What's the matter?"

"Nothing's the matter. I want to go. I had an experience a couple of weeks ago." She paused for a minute. "This is hard for me to explain, but I went to a church service and it felt good. I felt close to God."

"Terrific, Francie. If that makes you happy. It just seems strange." He shook his head. "I can't think of anyone in our family who's been religious."

"Maybe it's about time." She took a deep drink of diet soda. "I'd be happy if you'd like to come with me sometime." After she'd found a church.

"Yeah, sure, maybe sometime." He began to devour the enormous pile of French fries.

"How's your little brother doing?"

"I don't see Tim much. He's still living with the Montoyas."

"How long has he been with this foster family? Three years?"

"That's about right." He studied her frown. "Francie, stop worrying about him. Stop worrying about me. We're doing fine. With school and work, you've got enough to take care of in your life without taking on more."

She took one of his fries and studied him. "I'll never stop thinking about you. I'm just an old maid aunt who doesn't have any children of her own to watch after so I worry about you and Tim."

"You're the prettiest, youngest old maid aunt I've ever seen, but Tim's sixteen, almost grown up."

"Sixteen is *not* almost grown up. Sixteen just thinks it's almost grown up. So does twenty-one."

"I've been on my own for nearly four years and will be going to med school in the fall. If that isn't grown up, I don't know what is."

She smiled at him again just because he had matured into such a terrific young man.

"Now, don't get all teary-eyed," Mike warned.

"I wouldn't think about it, Mike. Anyway, I know you're still wet behind the ears, whether you believe it or not."

He shook his head as he finished off the last bite of hamburger. "My girlfriend—"

"Does she have a name?"

"Here's Cynthia's address." He handed her a small piece of paper. "She lives just north of the mall, in a pink house in the middle of the block."

That would be easy. Buses went to the mall all the time.

Mike stood. "I've got to run. Don't want

to be late for work." He turned toward Manny and Julie to say, "Thanks for lunch." Then he dropped a kiss on Francie's cheek and whispered, "I love you," before he ran out of the diner.

"Nice kid," Julie watched him as he walked out of the diner.

"Yeah, he is, isn't he?" Francie agreed. "I hope I can get him to come to church with me someday."

Chapter Three

"Would you look at the hunk that just came in?" Julie said to Francie as they served the lunch crowd the next week. "I'd trade Manny for him any day."

"In case you didn't realize it, you don't have Manny to trade," the cook shouted.

"Manny has to have the best ears in the world," Julie whispered. "Funny, when we were engaged, he never heard a word I said."

Francie grinned at Julie before turning to look at the man Julie had noticed. She promptly dropped the pitcher of iced tea she held. "Oh, my gosh. That's Mr. Fairchild."

"You know him? Who is he?" Julie grabbed a mop and started to clean up the puddle and broken glass.

"My parole officer." Francie knelt and began to pick up glass and ice cubes.

"Whoo-hoo! No wonder you called him a hunk! The man is gorgeous. And would you look at the suit? Handsome and tailored. My, my, my." She waved Francie away. "You go ahead and wait on him. I'll finish this. You want to show him how well you do your job."

"Oh, sure. Dropping that pitcher had to really impress him." She washed her hands and wiped them on her apron as she moved toward the booth where he sat. "May I take your order, Mr. Fairchild?"

"Do you have a menu?"

He looked completely out of place here. As Julie had said, his suit was beautiful. And yet he wore it casually, tossing the jacket over the back of the booth. He'd also unbuttoned the top of his shirt and loosened his tie.

Francie didn't think she'd ever seen a suit in here except the time Manny had worn one after his father's funeral, but Manny's suit was nothing like the one that covered Mr. Fairchild's broad shoulders.

Now, stop it, she lectured herself. A parolee should not be noticing how broad her parole officer's shoulders were, and, for goodness sake, she should not be drooling over someone so far out of her reach.

"A menu, please, Miss Calhoun?" he repeated.

"Oh, sure. Just a minute." She went to the cashier's booth, grabbed one and took it back to him. "Today's special is tuna salad sandwich with soup."

"That sounds nice. What's the soup?"

She went blank for a second. Why was she so nervous? She'd been a waitress for months, and remembering the specials didn't tax her intelligence all that often.

"Vegetable beef and chicken noodle," Julie shouted.

"And they aren't canned," Francie added. "Our cook makes them fresh every day."

"All right." He put down the menu. "I'll have a tuna sandwich with vegetable soup and a glass of tea."

Now if she could just bring him his food without dropping anything, most especially not Manny's hot vegetable soup on Mr. Fairchild's beautiful tan slacks.

When the order was up, she almost asked Julie to take it but reminded herself she could do this. She'd been waiting tables for almost six months, and he'd come to see *her* on the job.

With the bowl and plate in one hand and the glass of tea in the other and walking really slowly, she reached the booth, placed the food there, and didn't even spill a drop.

Standing back proudly, she said, "Will there be anything more?"

Brandon watched her from the moment he came in. She seemed nervous—dropping the pitcher was a sure sign—but he was used to his clients being anxious when he visited their work sites.

No, what he noticed was the fresh yellow uniform and ruffled white apron she wore, still with her old athletic shoes. She looked neat and bright and fresh, but it was her presence and smile that brought a little sunshine into the place, a bit of radiance that had nothing to do with the color of her uniform or the brilliance of the apron.

The customers liked her. She went from table to table, refilling glasses and taking orders, joking with some and listening to others. One of the men had tried to grab her. Quickly and unreasonably angry, Brandon had started out of the booth, but she had the situation in hand. She slipped away from the man with what looked like a practiced move and exchanged her smile for a glare—for just a second—to warn him. Very nicely done.

Why had he felt it was necessary to intervene when that man had tried to touch her? Well, she was his client and he should protect her, but he knew that wasn't the only reason. In fact, he refused to examine the thought any further and started to eat.

The food was surprisingly good; the soup hot, savory and full of meat and potatoes. The apple pie he ordered for dessert was delicious, juicy and sweet with a light, flaky crust. One of the best lunches he'd had in a long time.

He'd just taken his last bite of pie when the other waitress put two cups of coffee on the table and slid onto the bench opposite him.

"No, thank you, I don't need coffee," he started before she interrupted him.

"I'm Julie Sullivan. I own this place." She reached her hand out and shook his with a firm grip.

"Brandon Fairchild." He tried to stand in the narrow space but Julie put her hand on his shoulder and pushed him back down on the seat.

"I know who you are. When you came in, Francie told me your name and that you're her parole officer."

He opened his mouth to say he couldn't confirm that, but she continued.

"I know you can't tell me anything about Francie because that's all confidential."

He nodded and started to answer, but Julie swept on.

"But that doesn't stop me from telling you that she's a terrific kid. Conscientious, always at work on time, never misses a day *and* wants to improve herself. Did you know she's going to school?"

"Yes."

"Of course, you'd have that information. She's determined to do better than her family, not that that would take a lot of work. She wants to make something of herself and be a good example to her cousins."

"Her cousins?" Did he have any information about her cousins? He started to ask about them, but Julie started talking again and he'd already learned not to interrupt her.

"She loves those boys, has always tried to help with them. She's kept an eye on them all their lives, even when they were in foster homes after Tessie was caught." She fixed Brandon with a firm stare. "Francie's had a tough life but has never let it get her down although sometimes that's a struggle. You be nice to her," she warned.

"Thank you, Ms. Sullivan. It's good to know Miss Calhoun has such a good friend."

"You can't say a word about her, can you? It wouldn't be professional or ethical. You can't even say you'll be nice to her because that would show that you have a relationship, like being her parole officer, but that's okay. I just wanted you to know that, yes, Francie does have good friends." She moved her head in the direction of the kitchen. "Manny would do anything for her and so would I.

"Well, nice to meet you." She nodded and stood before reaching her hand out and shaking his again. "The meal's on the house."

"It was nice to meet you, also. And thank you, but I can't accept the meal." He took out his wallet and put a bill on the table.

"Oh, yeah." She picked up the money. "That'd be like a bribe, huh? Okay, I'll get you a receipt."

"What in the world did you say to him?" he heard Francie ask her boss.

"Don't you worry about it. Just take his change back to him and the receipt. Give him a big smile and maybe you'll get a good tip."

Miss Calhoun rolled her eyes but took the

change and receipt, brought them to the table and put them down in front of him.

"Thank you. I hope you enjoyed your lunch."

"It was very good. I'll recommend the diner to my friends."

"Yeah, Manny's a great cook."

For a moment, she just stood there, shifting from foot to foot before she said, "I'll see you next week." She picked up his dishes and smiled at him.

Her smile began with a slight hesitation before it turned into that high-voltage one she'd given him in his office. This time, he didn't turn away immediately or drop his eyes. This time, he watched her and basked— just for a moment wouldn't hurt anything— in the joy her expression brought him. Just for a moment, he allowed himself to soak in the warmth and happiness of her personality.

Then he reminded himself sternly that she was an ex-con and he was her parole officer and getting all sentimental because she had a wonderful smile was a really dumb and incredibly unethical thing to do.

But he grinned back at her before she turned and dumped the dirty dishes in a big plastic tub which very effectively destroyed the tenuous connection between them.

* * *

"Well," Julie said as she and Francie watched Mr. Fairchild leave, "you got yourself a great parole officer. He seems nice and professional."

"Ah," came Manny's voice from the kitchen. "You don't care if he's professional. All you care about is that he's good-looking."

"If I'd cared about men being good-looking, I never would have been engaged to you." She picked up a rag and started toward the empty tables.

"Then why were you engaged to me?" Manny put a plate on the dividing counter.

"I've never been able to figure it out."

Julie wiped the tables down with so much energy Francie was sure she'd throw her bad shoulder out, but she knew better than to interrupt a quarrel between her boss and the cook. Once she had. They'd both turned on her.

They were nice people, both of them, although Manny tried to act tough. Really nice people who had given her a job when she needed one. They'd never reminded her about her mistakes, about being an ex-con, just encouraged her and allowed her to work her schedule to get to classes.

They'd broken their engagement only days

after she started work. Both had pretended that it didn't bother them, that they hadn't been hurt or angry, but there was sure a lot of unresolved emotion hanging around.

That sounded like something she had picked up in psych class, didn't it?

Usually they didn't argue. Knowing how uncomfortable some of the customers would be with raised voices and fighting, Julie stayed in the diner and Manny in the kitchen. Both did their own tasks and pretended the other wasn't around. But every now and then their tempers exploded or a word was said and the other had to retaliate which made Francie feel as if she'd wandered onto a firing range.

Other times they were silent and glared at each other but the emotion was still there. It almost made the air crackle.

The whole thing upset her. It also reminded her that one fruit of the spirit was peace. She'd need to remember that, try to bring peace here, but she'd need a lot of help. Julie and Manny certainly weren't cooperating. They probably didn't want a ceasefire, much less a peace agreement.

"So, what are you doing this weekend?" Julie continued to clear and wipe tables while Francie completed the last few orders.

"What do I usually do? Go to class, study and sleep. But I'm excited about Sunday. I saw a church the other day when I was walking home from the bus stop."

"It just appeared, huh? Sort of a miracle?"

"No." Francie grinned at Julie's joke. "I'm sure it was always there but I just noticed it. It's a nice white building, not too big. It has a little steeple with a cross on top. It looks, well, like a church should look. Warm and welcoming. I thought I'd try it." She turned to look at Julie. "Want to come with me?"

"Hey, don't try this conversion thing with me. If you're happy, fine, but I haven't been to church for years and enjoy sleeping late Sunday morning."

"Well, if you ever change your mind—"

"Yeah, I'll be sure to tell you." Julie snorted.

Brandon glanced up from his paperwork at ten-thirty but didn't see Miss Calhoun in the reception area. Well, she wasn't late yet.

A few minutes later, Brandon looked at his watch again. She was four minutes late. Unusual, he thought. Not that he really knew. Nothing about her punctuality or lack of it had been written in her file, but her boss had mentioned it. In addition, he believed she wanted to impress him, to assure him she had changed.

After another minute, Brandon began to wonder again why he was so concerned about this one, about her. His other parolees could come an hour late, and he took advantage of the time by finishing up notes or making calls or seeing another client. Why did he care about Miss Calhoun? She was no different from the others, not a bit. Not one single bit, he repeated to himself.

Then she threw the door open and came into the office area. With one hand she closed the door. With the other she tried to tame her unruly curls. Unsuccessful at that, she dropped into a chair in the waiting area. Her remorse was so obvious he had to struggle not to smile.

He looked back at her file where he'd taken a few notes, questions he needed to ask her but the image of her, all the energy she radiated and those wild curls, stayed with him.

Brandon glanced up again. "Miss Calhoun?" he called.

Francie—Miss Calhoun, he corrected himself—stood and walked toward him. She wore jeans and a trim blue shirt with a button-down collar. A less buttoned-down person he'd never seen.

Did she have an extra spring in her step? Who in the world still used the phrase "spring in her step?" But she did seem to have a little more energy than when he'd seen her last.

"I'm sorry I'm late. I don't know what happened to the time."

"That's fine. You're only a few minutes late."

Standing, Brandon reached out his hand and shook hers. "Please sit down," he said as he did the same. For a moment, he shuffled the papers before he asked, "How has your week been?"

"Really terrific. I went to church last Sunday and think I found the right place."

"Why is that?"

"Well, as I told you before, I don't have a lot of clothes, especially not nice things to wear to church, but they didn't mind. Everyone greeted me and was so friendly. They even asked me to stay for their monthly dinner after the service. It was really great. They had me take home a plate of food for dinner." She paused for a moment. "And they take up an offering to help the hungry and homeless. Everyone brings canned food and beans and stuff."

"So they have a strong evangelism program and mission outreach."

She considered the words. "Yes, I guess that's what you'd call it, but it felt a lot friendlier."

"What about the minister?"

"He was really nice. It was a good sermon. I mean, if I could stay awake after school and work to listen, it had to be interesting."

"How was his theology?" What a dumb question. He was her parole officer. He was supposed to get her back on track, not act like a seminary professor. Or was he trying to put some space between them? Maybe even put her down to remind himself he knew more about church and religion than she did? Whatever the reason for the question, it wasn't at all necessary.

"Well, I have to tell you, I don't know. I liked what he said. He challenged me in some places, too—to be a better person."

Brandon looked down at his list of questions. "I need to set up a visit to your apartment."

"Oh?"

Because her voice sounded so horrified, he looked up at Miss Calhoun. Her eyes were wide and she was biting her lip.

"My apartment? Couldn't we meet someplace else?" she asked.

"No, Miss Calhoun. I have to make visits to the apartments of all my parolees." He motioned toward his list. "It's one of the requirements." He guessed she'd say Gentry hadn't done that so he repeated, "It is required."

She leaned forward. "It's just that I really don't want you—" she stopped and bit her lip again "or anyone to see my apartment."

"Is there a problem?" He started to write a note in her file.

"It's just not a really—" she paused as if she were searching for a word "—plush place," she finished. "It's little and not in a particularly nice area of town."

"Miss Calhoun, the people I work with don't come out of prison with a lot of money. I realize you can't afford much yet and that doesn't bother me. This is a purely professional visit."

"Oh, I know that. I'm really proud of how I've changed, except for the apartment."

"Miss Calhoun, most parolees don't want me to see where they live. They're embarrassed that where they live now is not as nice as they'd like. I know that, but I have to see that you do have a place to live."

After a long pause, she said, "Okay." Then she added, "You have my address. Do you know how to get there?"

He looked at her file. "Yes, I've had clients in that area before. Probably in that building. Do I remember that there's no elevator?"

She nodded. "My apartment's on the fourth floor. It isn't a bad climb."

"When is a good time?"

"That's harder to say. I work the breakfast and lunch shift, have classes Monday, Wednesday and Friday mornings and after-noons. The psych class is every afternoon."

"You don't work Saturdays?"

"No, we're only open during the week. We really serve people who work in the area. Some come for breakfast; a few stick around and work late. They drop in for dinner, but our big crowd is for lunch."

"You tell me. What day and time are best for you? I can change appointments around if I need to."

"Sometime between eight and ten Tuesday or Thursday?"

"Are you sure? I can work almost anything into my calendar."

"You certainly are flexible. Thanks, be-cause my schedule can be so crazy." She thought for a moment. "What about Tuesday?" That would give her the weekend to clean up. Not much to clean or make an improvement, but she'd try. "I don't have a class and can tell Julie I have to leave after breakfast. But I've got to be back at the diner by eleven."

"Eight-thirty? That way, I can come to your apartment first, before I come to the office. We'll both have plenty of time to get to work."

"Okay, that's fine."

He wrote the appointment on his calendar. "Do you need a card?"

"No, I'll remember."

"I need to get some information about your life and some dates, Miss Calhoun. The only one I have is the date of your birth."

"Go ahead."

"Parents' names?"

"Sam and Maisy Calhoun." She squirmed a little. "I don't like talking about my parents."

"Mother's maiden name?" he asked without a pause. She was like any other parolee, he reminded himself again. He couldn't ignore things she didn't like talking about—but he hated to see her so uncomfortable.

"Busby."

"Place of birth?"

"Me or them?"

"Yours, Miss Calhoun."

"I was born in Austin."

"Where are your parents now?"

"My father has been in Huntsville for—" she stopped to count "—for sixteen years. He should be out in a few years. As I told you earlier, I don't know anything about my mother since she left, and I don't remember much of her before she walked out."

"And you haven't heard from her?" He continued to take notes and fill in blanks on the information sheet.

"Not a word since she left." She looked down at her hands. "I'll never understand that. I've always wondered how a woman could walk out on a child without making arrangements for her care."

He wished he could say something reassuring but thought she'd probably feel uncomfortable if he did. Besides, this was all purely professional. "Then you went to live with your uncle, Louis Calhoun?"

"Yes, and after he was incarcerated for grand theft auto, I lived with my aunt Tessie, Tessie Fuller."

"Your boss mentioned you have two cousins. Are they Mrs. Fuller's children?"

Francie nodded.

"What are their names?"

She shifted in her seat. "Why do you need to know that?"

"Gentry kept no information on any of his clients. I could pull up the prison records but they're not always complete. Are you uncomfortable with this? Do you mind helping me complete this information?" He glanced up at her.

"No, but my cousins aren't involved in the family business—you know, crime—and I don't like to include them in this. I'm sort of protective of them. Can't you leave their names out?"

"Miss Calhoun, this is purely informational, for my files."

She took a deep breath and sat back in the chair. "Okay," she said reluctantly. "My nephews are Mike—he's twenty-one—and Tim. He's sixteen and lives with a foster family. Mike did, too, until he was seventeen. Mike will graduate from college this spring. He's going to be a doctor." She smiled. "They're great young men."

"Very impressive." He wrote a few more notes before looking at her. "What's your phone number?"

"I don't have a phone but the woman down the hall will take messages." She gave him that number and those of her cousins.

"Any other relatives?"

"Not that I know of. I don't know if my mother had family." She bit her lip and looked away. "I mean after she left us."

"Thank you. That should fill in everything." He studied the form again. "Oh, one more thing. How's your health?"

"Fine. No problems."

He closed the folder and handed her a card. "Here's the name of the financial aid officer at your school. I talked to her. She said for you to come in. She believes they can help you with tuition and books."

"Oh, how wonderful." She looked as if he'd given her a wonderful gift. "Even a little bit would make so much difference. I wouldn't have to feel like I'm always broke." She rubbed her hand across her jeans. "I could buy some new shoes and maybe a dress to wear to church." They were such small things, but she glowed with pleasure at the idea.

"I hope it works out."

"And thank you." She scooted forward in the chair. "Thank you for doing this. I wish you'd been my parole officer from the beginning."

Then she directed her smile toward him. He felt warm inside, a sensation a truly professional parole officer should not feel—and he never had before—when one of his clients smiled.

Today he'd made an effort to be warmer, in a professional way. When he'd erected the front of cold indifference previously he'd felt as if he'd hurt her deeply. His inability to be objective, his tendency to see her as an attractive woman, not a parolee, were his fault, not hers. No, he couldn't be her good buddy.

How much longer he could continue to work with Miss Calhoun?

What an odd thought. He pushed it away. Structure and firmness were the best way to keep a relationship with a parolee proper and professional, he reminded himself.

"Thank you, Miss Calhoun. If there isn't anything more?"

"Oh, no, thank you." She stood.

"I'll see you Tuesday."

"Yes, thank you. Tuesday." She smiled at him, that smile that warmed him, before she left the cubicle.

Then Mitzi Matthews—a seasoned criminal of fifty with the hard expression of a

woman who'd been in trouble all her life—
took Miss Calhoun's place.

If he had anything to do with it, Miss Calhoun would never end up like Mitzi Matthews.

Chapter Four

The entire weekend—except for the time Francie went to church or studied or the few hours on Sunday afternoon when she went to Mike's girl friend's barbecue—she cleaned. She swept and mopped and then swept and mopped again.

Finally, she spent almost an entire afternoon on her hands and knees with a scrub brush and bucket of sudsy water, scouring off the dirt of decades. There was residue built up in the corners she was sure no one had ever touched. She had to dig it out with a toothbrush and a nail file.

Using vinegar and a newspaper, she polished the window until it shown, but, since the view was so dismal, she pulled down the shade. The poor thing was covered with spots of dirt and scrapes, but she discovered correction fluid covered them up pretty well.

Tuesday morning she rushed back from work to do another quick cleaning. She stood in the middle of the small room and turned in a slow circle to make sure she had scrubbed or swept or polished every square inch.

Not that the little place took all that much time, but she did want it sparkling and immaculate because it would never be spacious and beautiful or even attractive.

After straightening one of the glorious paintings that covered the dingy wallpaper, she moved back to survey the room. It was the best she could do, she thought as she squared the yellow tablecloth and tugged the quilt that covered the worn back of the sofa bed.

She wished she could hide the burned place on the linoleum, but short of putting a piece of furniture in the middle of the floor, there was nothing she could do.

She took a deep sniff and could still smell the roach killer she'd used to get rid of the horrible crawly creatures. She knew from experience they wouldn't stay away long. The next time one of her neighbors fumigated, they'd be back and she'd have to fumigate again.

To get rid of as much of the odor as possible, she threw the window open, then checked the weather. It was always dark in the alley but she could see clear sky if she leaned out way too far and looked up.

She switched on the floor fan in the corner which began to move the air around. That should be okay for now. It was morning and not all that hot yet although the forecast for that afternoon was ninety degrees.

Forcing herself to admit she'd done everything she could to brighten the apartment, Francie washed her hands, changed her T-shirt and combed her hair. That completed, Francie took three steps to the center of the apartment and began to pace.

Francie was *not* a patient person. That was something she had to work on. After all, it was the fourth fruit of the spirit. She would work on patience soon, but not now, not yet. She was way too nervous for that.

She made herself sit and relax on the sofa as she thought about church and how friendly and welcoming the members were.

The barbecue on Sunday afternoon had been wonderful. Cynthia was lovely—pretty and pleasant. Her family had welcomed Francie, fed her a delicious meal with ribs and potato salad. They'd even driven her back to her apartment in the late afternoon and hadn't commented on the terrible area of town Francie lived in. Once there, they'd waited until she got inside the building before driving off.

Francie could tell how Mike felt about Cynthia, hovering around her, gently touching her hand or her back, bringing her a soft drink when she needed one. Cynthia had gazed at Mike as if he was the most wonderful man in the world, as, of course, he was.

Wasn't love great? Well, she didn't really know. She'd never been in love. Oh, she'd dated, although not much and not recently. She'd never been in love before. Was that because of her problems or because the few times she'd dated she always picked losers? Must be another hereditary characteristic. She hoped her cousins had missed this one.

When she heard a knock at the door, she flew off the sofa and stood hyperventilating in the middle of the small room. She calmed herself down by repeating, "The fruit of the spirit is love, joy, peace, patience..." as she moved toward the door and opened it.

There Mr. Fairchild stood, all six feet plus of him, dressed in a soft blue shirt, blue patterned tie and blue slacks. No jacket today. Probably wise, with the heat.

At that moment it struck her why it had been so important for her to clean up the apartment, why she hadn't wanted him to see the dump in the first place, knowing it would give him such a bad impression of her.

The reason was simple: she didn't think of him as only her parole officer. As a woman, she saw him as an attractive man, of course. Any woman would see Mr. Fairchild as a man, an incredibly handsome man. Obviously she was no different from them.

His blond hair was neatly combed this time—he probably hadn't had time to rumple it the way he did at work—and his gray eyes looked friendly, for a moment, before he again shuttered them.

Moving through the door and past Francie, he studied the tiny space. It didn't take long.

"Very neat and clean, Miss Calhoun."

When she started to close the door to the hall, he said, "Please leave it open."

She did.

That taken care of, he turned to study the apartment again. "Look at those paintings. Aren't they beautiful? It must be great to live surrounded by them."

Of course the pictures had caught his attention. How could they not? The colors and the feeling of sunlight that radiated from them turned anyone's thoughts from the grubby room.

"Thank you."

"Where did you get these? They are marvelous." He scrutinized a painting of a young woman walking through a field of brilliant red poppies.

"My Aunt Tessie painted them. I had them in storage until I found a place to live."

"A very talented woman. Too bad she didn't paint her own pictures."

"Yes, but the sad truth is she didn't have a style of her own. When she tried, her paintings weren't at all pretty. They never sold, but she could imitate anyone's style." She pointed to the canvases around them. "My favorites were always the Impressionists. Aren't they lovely?"

"Beautiful, but it's too bad she didn't stick to painting in their style and selling under her name."

"Yes." Francie sighed. "Aunt Tessie said the idea of honesty sounds good, but it doesn't put food on the table. She could make thousands of dollars more with a forgery than with one of her originals." She held up her hand. "And, yes, I know it was shortsighted because she ended up in prison, but that was her philosophy. Oh, not going to prison but putting food on the table for her family."

"You're keeping the paintings for her?"

"For her and for my cousins. I promise these will never be sold as Renoirs or Monets. And I assure you that I have warned my cousins many times that crime doesn't pay. Their mother and I are good—or bad—examples of that."

"Fine." He nodded as he moved around the room, looked out the window and wandered toward the kitchenette. "How long have you lived here?"

"Six months." She watched him turn around again. "Is everything all right? Is there anything else?"

"Do you have canceled checks to show you have been paying rent here?"

She blinked. "Do you mean, to show I live here? I assure you I do." She pushed the curtain of the small closet back. "See, all my clothes are here." Although they were pitifully few.

"Miss Calhoun, you would be amazed at the tricks some ex-cons pull to make me believe they are straight and living in one apartment, when actually they have returned to crime and are living somewhere with associates that violate their parole. I believe you, but I need proof."

"Okay. I don't have checks because we have to pay cash but I have the receipts." She went to one of the three kitchen drawers and pushed its contents around before she pulled out several tattered pieces of paper.

"I don't have them all right here, although I could probably find the rest if you need them." She handed them to him one at a time. "This is for this month and this one is for last month and this one is for the first month I was here."

"These are fine." He wrote a note on a pad he pulled from his pocket then handed them back. "Very good, Miss Calhoun. I can't think of anything more."

She watched him expectantly.

"You have done very well here. You've created a warm and pleasant atmosphere. The fact that you have made this room a home makes me optimistic that you're going to continue to do well in your rehabilitation."

"Thank you."

Oh, his having confidence in her made her feel so good that she wanted to grab his hand and dance around to show her pleasure. She reined her enthusiasm in. He still had that slightly distant expression that warned her off. And he was, she reminded herself again, her parole officer. Not her good friend. Not her boyfriend.

Instead, she smiled and said, "Thank you," again.

Suddenly the room became smaller and Mr. Fairchild, who was almost three feet away, seemed very close, much too close.

In his eyes, there was that look again, the gaze she had once believed showed interest, maybe even attraction. Suddenly and unexpectedly she was aware of his presence, of his overwhelming masculinity, of a faint spicy scent and the way he seemed to be leaning toward her, just a little, but it was definitely a tilt in her direction.

It made her very nervous at the same time she yearned to reach toward him.

They stood there, gazing at each other but not moving for several seconds before Mr. Fairchild stepped back and blinked.

"Is there anything else?" she asked softly.

He shook his head. "No," he said as he turned hastily toward the open door. "I'll see you next Thursday at your usual time."

"Yes, sir." Then she said, "Thank you," again because she didn't know what else to say.

"You're welcome." He stepped into the hall.

She watched him as he walked down the hall and started down three flights of steps. When she couldn't see him anymore, Francie closed the door and sat down at the table.

What had happened? She couldn't even guess. After all, Mr. Fairchild wouldn't be, would never be, interested in Francie Calhoun, not with her family and her background. He'd never care about a woman who'd held up a convenience store and spent time behind bars, a woman who worked in a diner and lived in this apartment, who wore cheap clothes and ratty shoes.

But he hadn't hated the place. That was good. Although it must be smaller and much uglier than where he lived, he'd said she'd made it warm and pleasant, like a home.

She would have to forget those few seconds, the surprising connection between them. She had to remind herself what a generous and kind man Mr. Fairchild was. Both of those were certainly fruit of the spirit.

But she was fairly sure she was drawn to much more about Mr. Fairchild than any evidence of the fruit of the spirit.

Because Julie had stayed home sick on Wednesday and Thursday, Francie'd had to work late to cover the dinner crowd and had been run off her feet trying to take care of the lunch crew alone. Her day ran from setting up for breakfast at five-thirty in the morning to eight at night when Manny ran her off while he cleaned up. On top of that add studying and working on a paper, and she was exhausted.

So it didn't surprise Francie when she fell asleep over her books late Thursday night. At midnight, she'd stood, stretched and meandered toward the sofa, not even bothering to open it into a bed. Pulling her shoes and jeans off, she fell onto the cushions, pulled the blanket over her and fell asleep immediately.

What did surprise Francie was that she slept until eleven the next morning.

Oh, no! She'd missed breakfast—Hank, the morning cook, would have been there alone—and was going to miss half an hour of the lunch shift. She hoped Julie was back or Manny would have to do everything himself until she got there.

Running into the bathroom, she showered and brushed her hair and teeth before she threw on her jeans and T-shirt. Then she pulled her shoes on, grabbed her purse and ran out of the apartment.

It was almost eleven-thirty when she arrived at the diner, running the entire way.

"What happened to you, kid?" Julie said when Francie burst through the door.

Francie leaned over to catch her breath. "I'm sorry. I overslept."

"Hank called me. He said the crowd was light this morning and his daughter came in to help. She can use the tips."

"I'm so sorry, Julie." Finally able to breathe normally, she straightened and said. "And I missed class, too."

"Yeah, we know." Julie turned to seat three men at a booth.

"How could you know that?"

"Mr. Fairchild called."

"Oh, no." She moaned inside. "Why? How would he know?"

"I'll explain that later, okay? First we've got to feed these people." She took out her order pad.

Francie changed into her uniform, grabbed her apron and started waiting tables.

When the crowd dwindled, Julie said, "Mr. Fairchild said he went to observe you in class but you weren't there. He wants you to call at two o'clock."

"Wouldn't you know. He came to the one

class I've missed all semester." Francie placed a hamburger in front of her customer. "Thanks for taking the message."

She studied Julie for a second. "You know, you look really tired and pale. Are you all right?"

"She shouldn't have come back," Manny shouted. "Stubborn woman was really sick."

"He brought me soup," Julie whispered. "Don't tell him you know. He'd hate to admit he can be a softie."

"She should have stayed home another day, rested all weekend and come back on Monday, but you can't tell her anything," Manny continued, slapping a hamburger with the spatula.

"I'm fine. Just a little tired but I'm not at all contagious," she said.

"Julie, you take care of yourself. Why don't you sit down?" Francie motioned toward a chair. "I'll finish serving everyone else and clean up."

"Good idea. You know, Julie," Manny spoke slowly and clearly to his boss, "you're not as young as you think you are. You need to rest when you can."

"Thanks, Manny. How old are you? Forty-three?" Julie said. "I'll sit down and rest, but keep your thoughts about my age to yourself."

Julie did rest, which worried Francie. Julie never slowed down, never relaxed, but today she settled on the bench of an empty booth, her back against the wall and her legs stretched out in front of her. Within two minutes, she'd fallen asleep.

When Francie looked at her again after serving the last table, Julie had a blanket over her and Manny had just returned to the kitchen. He gave her a glare that warned Francie not to say a word about what he'd done and went back to cleaning the range while Francie wiped the tables.

At two, Francie called the number Mr. Fairchild had left. On the second ring, he answered with, "Fairchild."

"Mr. Fairchild, this is Francie Calhoun."

"Yes, Miss Calhoun. I visited your class this morning. You weren't there."

"That's right, sir. I'm afraid I overslept. This has been a very busy week with my boss sick and finals and a paper to write. I fell asleep last night while I was studying and forgot to set the alarm. I don't usually miss."

There was a silence that sounded very judgmental on the other end.

"I don't, Mr. Fairchild," she hurried to explain. "This is the first time I've missed all semester. Besides, in college, they don't care if you miss as long as you do the work."

"But *I* care, Miss Calhoun. I expect you to attend every class, especially if you get financial aid next semester. Missing class and appointments is a habit you do not want to get into."

"Of course not, sir. I haven't missed any appointments and don't plan to."

"Good." He paused. "I need to ask you a favor. I had to set up a job-site visit during your regular time. Could you come in on Thursday next week? At ten?"

"Sure, that would be fine."

"Great, I'll see you Thursday."

"Yes, sir, and thank you for visiting class. It must keep you very busy checking on me at all these places, but I appreciate your interest."

"It's all part of the job, Miss Calhoun. Besides, I don't have to check on all my parolees as I do you. Many of them don't have jobs, unfortunately, and most of them are not in school. I wish all of them were as active in their rehabilitation as you are."

"Thank you." The compliment warmed her inside. "Goodbye."

Why did his words make her feel good? The fact that she was a good parolee wasn't a big thing as the world measured success. Being a parolee was actually a measure of failure, but his kind words pleased her anyway. She hadn't gotten all that many in her life. Of course, she hadn't deserved many.

"Did it go okay? Are you in trouble?" Manny asked, a worried look in his dark eyes. "Sounded like you had to do a lot of explaining."

"It was fine. You know I don't usually miss stuff—work or school or appointments, but Mr. Fairchild has to follow up on it. He wants to make sure his parolees make it."

"Well, Francie, I don't have any doubt that you will. *No cabe duda.*"

"Thanks, Manny."

After Brandon hung up the phone, he saw Sean McCray waiting in the reception area. The sight of Sean—so determined and hardworking—made Brandon smile. He waved for the young man to come over.

"How are things going, Mr. McCray?"

"Fine, Mr. Fairchild."

Brandon studied Sean while the young man talked. He seemed like a nice kid. He had honest brown eyes, freckles and neatly combed brown hair. His clothing was clean but worn, like that of most ex-cons.

He'd gotten in with the wrong crowd after high school and spent a few years in prison because of it.

"Mr. Fairchild," he said, leaning forward. His eyes flashed with excitement. "I have an interview this afternoon at the Burger Bar. I think I have a good chance to get this job."

Brandon listened and took a few notes. "We've had good luck placing parolees there.

"If I get it, I can arrange my hours so I can go to technical school. I'd like to become an electrician. They make good money. It's honest work."

"What about those friends of yours?" Brandon studied the file. "Jorge Barrios and Chester Robertson?"

"I don't see them anymore, Mr. Fairchild. I learned my lesson. They can get in trouble if they want to, but I'm going straight."

"Glad to hear that." Brandon stood and shook Sean's hand. "Let me know about that job. I'll see you in two weeks. We can talk about vocational training then."

Yes, the kid was going to make it. He had goals and the drive and the ambition to get what he wanted in life. If he had to bet on anyone to make it, it would be Sean Mc-Cray—and Miss Calhoun.

Sometimes there were good things about this job. Those two made him feel it was worthwhile. He wished all parolees were more like them.

However, never missing an appointment wasn't as easy at it sounded, Francie realized on Thursday of the next week, when she was supposed to meet with Mr. Fairchild again.

She's promised Julie she'd work breakfast so Julie could sleep in.

"What are you doing here?" Francie asked, surprised to see Manny instead of the usual breakfast cook.

"Hank called me at home, said he was sick and couldn't come in."

"Now you're working an extra shift?" She tied her apron on.

"If I'd told Julie, she would have come in and cooked, and you know what a terrible cook she is."

"I don't think that's the reason, Manny. Julie's a great cook. Not as good as you, of course."

"Yeah, well who is?"

"Nobody, but I know you're here so she can sleep in, right?"

"Silly woman, she still isn't well," Manny complained as he put an order up. "I told her to go to the doctor but she says she's feeling better. She always ignores any advice I give her."

"You're a good guy, Manny." Francie delivered the plate, then came back for coffee and juice. "You try to hide it by being tough, but you're really a nice guy."

He ignored her words. "Julie still thinks she's thirty, but she's going on fifty and won't slow down," he said shaking his head. "She should get more help, take more time off, not work as hard."

"Can she afford to do that, Manny?"

"Better than killing herself, isn't it? She could shut down after lunch, maybe two o'clock. We don't make that much extra money for dinner. It'd give her an easier life, but will she?" He pressed down so hard on the bacon he was cooking that grease shot up and splattered his apron. "Of course not."

"She likes her work, Manny."

"Does she likes running her legs off waiting on people, working so hard she gets really sick?" He glowered at Francie.

Francie didn't bother to answer. When she came back to the dividing counter between the kitchen and the diner to hang up an order, he hadn't stopped talking.

"What do you do with a stubborn woman like that? She won't listen to a word anyone says, won't take a word of advice, just pushes and pushes herself. Someday." He waved his spatula at Francie. "Someday she's going to work so hard she'll hurt herself. Then what? Who'll take care of her then? She doesn't have a family. She works too hard to have many friends."

Francie picked up her order. "Who would take care of her? We would, Manny, and you know it. Those of us who love her would take care of Julie if she needed us."

Manny's face paled and his mouth dropped open. "I'm not saying I *love* the woman. I just worry about her. I mean, if she dies, I'm out of a job."

Francie turned so he couldn't see her smile. "Okay, those of us who *worry* about her would take care of her. Besides, Manny, you're such a good cook, you could get a job any place you wanted to, making more money than you make here. That's why I doubt you worry about her health to keep you in a job."

He frowned at her and turned back to his stove.

"In fact," Francie added, "I wonder why you stay here working for a boss you always fight with."

When he didn't answer, she took another order and clipped it up while she picked up a plate of toast. "You know, I don't think Julie's going to wear out soon. She just got sick and she can't get over it. She'll be fine if we can get her to rest."

Manny didn't look convinced. He didn't say another word aloud, but Francie could hear him mumbling softly, "Never said I *loved* the woman, never said anything like that."

Once the business regulars who stopped for breakfast had finished and left, the crowd got lighter. A couple of high-school kids who were skipping first period, Francie guessed, a few elderly couples from the retirement village around the corner who dropped in for coffee every day and a sprinkling of accountants and secretaries on their breaks. Not a hard job to serve them.

At nine o'clock, Officer Ricardo Lester

came in. He usually had a big smile for everyone, but this morning his face was drawn into an expression of concern. Francie thought that couldn't be good.

"Francie, can I see you a minute?" He led her toward an isolated booth.

Oh, oh. She *knew* this couldn't be good. "Do you want coffee?" she asked.

When he shook his head, she slid into the booth across from him.

"Listen, Francie, this is really hard to tell you."

"My cousins, Mike and Tim, are they okay? Was there an accident? Are they in the hospital?"

"No, no. They're okay far as I know, but there's something else."

She knew this had to be about her cousins because, well, there was no one else in her life. After taking a deep breath and closing her eyes for a quick request to God for courage, she looked at the officer again.

"There's word out on the street that Tim bought a gun last night, a Saturday-night special." The officer shook his head.

"He bought *what?* Where?"

"A gun, from the trunk of a guy's car. That's why we were really concerned."

"Are you sure? I mean, that it was Tim?"

"As sure as we can be." He nodded slowly. "We've heard about it from a couple of sources so we think it's probably true."

"Why in the world would Tim need a gun?" Francie shook her head, but she knew. Oh, yeah, Tim was feeling the pull of his genetic predisposition and had decided to act on it.

"I'm not even going to guess what's going on with him, Francie, but the fellows and I thought you should know." He looked up at her. "I know you're on parole, but maybe, somehow, you could get the gun away from him before he decides to do something foolish. You know, just in case the kid's mind was running in that direction."

Of course Tim's mind was running in that direction. Why else would he buy a gun? "Thank you, officer."

"We all admire what you're doing with your life, Francie. All your hard work. We'd hate to see that kid you care so much about make a mistake." He stood.

"It is a worry, officer."

"Like I said, we don't have any reason to arrest him. It's not a big enough offense to spend any time on. Yeah, he's young, and he shouldn't have a gun, but I'll leave that up to you."

She nodded again. "Thank you. Now I have to figure out what do." She forced herself to smile up at the officer. "I appreciate this. I will take care of it. Somehow."

But how?

After he left, Francie sat in the booth for a few more minutes thinking. *She* was on probation. She couldn't touch a gun, couldn't even take it away from Tim. What was she going to do?

Well, there actually was no choice. It didn't matter what happened to her, but Tim couldn't get in trouble. She wouldn't allow it. For years, she'd been working hard to keep Mike and Tim from making the same mistakes their relatives had, from ruining their lives. She wasn't about to stop now, just because it could land her back in prison.

Francie stood and looked into the kitchen. "Manny, I have to go. I've got to do something, but I can't tell you what. It's important."

"Yeah, I'd guess so if a cop delivered the message." But Manny didn't asked for more information. He just nodded. "It's late and the crowd's small. I can take care of it by myself this morning. Could you take the coffee around before you leave while I finish this order?"

"I'm sorry to leave you alone."

"It's okay, Francie. You wouldn't do it if it wasn't an emergency."

Francie picked up the coffeepot and went from table to table, filling cups, all the time anxious and worried. By the time she'd finished, her hand shook.

She brewed another pot of coffee and put it down on the warmer, willing herself not to shake any more. She didn't even bother to change out of her uniform but tossed on her sweater.

"Bye, Manny, and thanks. Tell Julie I'll try to be here on time for lunch." She paused. "I hope Julie's well enough to be here."

"Hey, don't worry. We both know you'll be here when you can."

She gave him a quick wave before running out the door and toward the bus stop.

It took twenty minutes by bus to get to the subdivision where Tim lived with the Montoyas, his foster family. It was a nice neighborhood with small but comfortable houses, mature trees and small gardens.

Of course, Tim *should* be in school, but she'd check the house first. If she needed to, she could find him at school but had a feeling he wouldn't be there. If he'd bought a gun, he was in a dangerous mood. If he were really angry, getting in trouble for missing school probably wouldn't bother him at all.

And, oh, how she hoped he hadn't taken the gun to school.

Not surprisingly, no one answered the front door. Both foster parents worked and their two young children were in school.

The house looked deserted, but she couldn't give up. She walked around the side of the house, studying the windows, leaning back to look up at the partly open window of Tim's room, but the room was dark behind the screen and half-drawn blinds. Dark and silent.

She listened but could hear nothing inside the house. Sort of silly, really, because Tim's room was on the second floor so how would she know if he was there? But she didn't hear the loud crashes of his favorite music to help her locate him.

Was she going to have to pull him out of school to discuss this? Oh, she didn't want to have to. People would remember that. She'd have to talk to someone in the office, maybe a principal, to get to see Tim. Word would get back to his foster family and maybe the case worker. Who could guess where it might end up? Perhaps Mr. Fairchild would discover she'd had a gun.

Oh, my, Mr. Fairchild. She'd completely forgotten Mr. Fairchild.

She glanced at her watch. It was a quarter to ten. Looked like she'd miss her appointment. She hated that. Mr. Fairchild would be furious, sure she was manipulating him again, positive she was trying to sabotage her rehabilitation. She'd lose his confidence. Yes, that would hurt, but she did have priorities. Tim was one of the most important.

Was there music coming from the garage? She thought so. As quietly as possible, Francie moved to the other side of the house and toward the detached garage until she could see inside. Yes, Tim was there, sitting in the car his foster family allowed him to drive, the radio on, the open with his left foot hanging out.

In his hands, he held the gun. At least, she though he held a gun. She couldn't see it well from here, but he was looking down at something shiny and metallic, caressing it. Calhoun men often fell deeply in love with their weapons, another trait she'd like to break them of.

"Oh, dear God, give me love and patience

and self-control," she whispered. *"And a lot of wisdom would be much appreciated."*

Silently, she moved toward the car. When she got close enough, she said, "Tim?"

Her cousin turned toward her, his face distorted with fear and anger. He did hold a gun, a silver-colored Saturday-night special.

And, in his shaking hands, the gun was pointed right at her.

She hoped it wasn't loaded.

Chapter Five

"Francie, what are you doing here?" Tim dropped the gun onto his lap and tried to act as though he hadn't pointed it at his cousin, tried to pretend the weapon wasn't even there.

"Hey, Tim, I just thought I'd come over to see you." Francie said as she opened a lawn chair and settled herself next to the open door of the car.

"Shouldn't you be working or at school?" Tim's voice trembled. He cleared his throat. "I mean, instead of being here?" He glanced at her then back at his lap. "Why are you here?"

Francie studied her younger cousin for a minute. Tim was thin, almost skinny, and shorter than most sixteen-year-old boys, exactly like Mike had been at that age. He had short dark hair and looked a lot like both Mike and her when they were sixteen.

And he had an innocent face, the kind of open face the Calhouns used for their con games. If she hadn't known all the tricks, his expression might've made her forget the gun in his lap.

"Manny let me leave early so I thought I'd drop by."

"Drop by?" Tim rolled his eyes. "This is ten miles from any place you'd be."

She continued to speak conversationally. "Shouldn't you be at school? What time does your first class start?"

"Oh, soon." He laid his hand over the gun and reached for the keys as though he was going to turn the engine on and back out.

Did he really think she hadn't noticed the weapon? Well, she decided it would be best to keep him wondering if she would mention it. Let him worry. "Really? I thought it would begin before ten o'clock."

"Oh, yeah, I'm going in a little late today."

"Do the Montoyas know that? That you're going in a little late?"

"Um, no." He paused and rubbed his fingers across his eyes. "Um, after they left for work, I got to feeling sick. In my stomach."

He put a hand there. "Yeah, in my stomach. I feel a lot better now so I'll get going." He reached into his pocket and pulled out his keys, careful not to jar the gun.

"Why are you in such a hurry to go?" Francie asked. "I just got here."

"I'm already late for school."

"So a few more minutes won't make much difference." She settled back in the chair while he dropped the keys on the seat next to him.

"Okay, what do you want to talk about?" He didn't look at Francie or seemed the slightest bit happy either to see her or that she wouldn't leave.

"How's school?" she asked the side of his head.

"Okay."

"And the Montoyas? Are they treating you well? Is living here still all right?"

"Okay. I mean, they're okay and living here is okay. Everything's okay."

Was there anything harder than trying to pry information from a teenager who didn't want to talk?

"I envy you," she said after an endless minute of silence.

"Oh, sure."

"Well, look at me. You've got new shoes—looks like a good brand—and designer jeans and I don't. Must be nice to get that."

"Francie, there are more important things than nice clothes. You always tell me that."

"On top of that, you go to a great high school, clean and big."

He nodded.

"I didn't go to high school after your mother was sent to prison."

"Yeah, I know." He still couldn't meet her eyes, kept them down on the gun in his lap.

"I was in a juvenile facility for two years. I didn't want to be there, but I thought I was too smart to be caught. On top of that, I didn't want to go to school—still thought I was too smart—so I flunked everything. You know, they couldn't make me do anything, certainly couldn't force me to learn."

"Not too bright."

"No, I wasn't. I thought I was really smart, but I wasn't." She paused and studied his face. During the short time she'd been there, he'd developed a little tic in his left cheek. "How are your grades?"

"Okay."

"Tim, how are your grades?"

"They really are okay." He glanced over at

her. "Honest. Mostly Bs, some As, a C in Spanish, but that's hard."

"Are you on track to graduate next year?"

He nodded.

"Tim," she said quietly with all the love and patience and gentleness she could put in her words, "why did you buy the gun?"

"How did you know I had a gun?" Tim shouted.

When she didn't answer, he looked away.

"Are there problems at school?"

He gazed at her again, a question in his eyes before he looked back down at the gun.

"Do they beat you up because you're small?"

"Why would you think that?" This time his head snapped up and he met her eyes.

"Because kids do. Bullies in all situations pick on smaller people. When I was in prison, I was easy prey. I got beaten up all the time. Broken ribs, bruises."

"All the time, Francie?"

"All the time," she repeated. "I know what it's like. It happened in juvie, too, but more in prison."

"Well, I'm tired of it." Tim shook his head, his lip jutted out in front. "I'm not going to take it anymore. No, I'm not going to take it," he repeated.

"Instead you're going to take a gun and blow them all away?"

"Francie, you know I wouldn't do that. I'm going to frighten them. Just show the gun around, scare them a little so they'll leave me alone."

"What's going to happen to you when the principal finds you have a gun in school?"

"He won't."

"Tim," she said, forcing her voice to stay low and calm, "what would happen if the principal found out you had a gun in school?"

"I'd be suspended. Maybe arrested."

"And you might be put in a juvie facility, which, I have to tell you, is far worse than high school. You have to trust me on that."

He looked at the gun. She knew she hadn't convinced him, not yet.

"Maybe thinking about pulling a job with it?"

Again he said nothing, but his expression showed her he had.

"That would really show the guys at school that you're tough, wouldn't it?"

He nodded.

"The police know you have a gun."

"They do? How do they know?" His eyes narrowed. "Did you snitch on me?"

"No, a cop told me about the gun. They know you have it. If anything goes down in this neighborhood, who do you think they'll suspect first?"

He didn't answer.

"Have I mentioned that you don't want to be in a juvie facility? You couldn't play soccer or run to a movie whenever you wanted or take those upper-level classes you want for college."

He shrugged.

"Tim," she leaned forward to stare at him as she spoke clearly, "you *will* be beaten at least once or twice a week, I guarantee that."

He looked up at her, eyes wide.

"Yes, at least once or twice a week, maybe more with men, I don't know."

"But wouldn't the guards keep that from happening?"

"No." She gave a mirthless laugh. "No one will ever get in trouble for it. The guards won't see a thing. It's too much trouble and paperwork. If you snitch, it'll get worse. No one will help you. No one will tell the guards what happened, even if that would help. You're never as alone as you are in prison."

"But I hate school, Francie. I hate it. I'm so small. I look like a baby. I'm really tired of getting beaten up and laughed at."

"Tim, I don't have a solution for that. All I can tell you is that I know *your* solution will only make things worse. I've been there."

"I know, but—"

"Can you avoid these guys?"

"Not when I'm in a gym with them. Not when I have to walk down the hall to class." He shook his head. "It's really bad, like you said, Francie, and if I complain, it'd be worse."

"Tim, you have less than two years of school left. When you're in college, this won't happen. Heck, when you're a senior, it might get better. Some of those guys will be gone and you'll probably grow. Mike started his growth spurt when he was your age."

"Yeah." He looked down at his feet. "I noticed my jeans are a little shorter."

"I don't know what I can say, but I love you, and I don't want you to go through what I have."

"I know, Francie."

"I don't want you to go to jail." She watched him for a few seconds. "Now, give me the gun."

His fingers clenched it. "Why? I won't use it. I'll lock it in my drawer, with the ammunition out."

"Tim, I don't want you to be tempted, and I don't want someone else to get hold of it and commit a crime that would implicate you."

"No, Francie."

She waited silently while he rubbed the barrel of the gun.

"You can't take the gun," he said. "That would break your probation."

"I can handle that." She held out her hand. "It'll be better for you to let me have it."

He sat and looked at the gun, still gently rubbing his fingers over the weapon's silvery surface until, grudgingly, he picked it up and handed it to Francie. "What are you going to do with it?"

"I don't know." She couldn't take it to the police. She'd have to toss it where no one would find and use it. "First, I want you to dump the bullets then get me a plastic bag and a cloth so I can clean your fingerprints off them and the gun."

Once she had those, Francie carefully wiped the gun and bullets while she avoided covering the surface with her prints. Then she wrapped the rag around the gun, placed it in the bag, squeezed all the air out of the bag that she could and tucked the package in the large pocket of her uniform. She wrapped the bullets in a tissue and shoved that packet in the other pocket.

Finished with that, Francie stood and took Tim's hand to pull him out of the car. After enfolding him in a big hug, she said, "I love you. Don't let stuff get to this level, when you're about to explode." She looked him in the eyes. "You know you can talk to me, don't you?"

"I know, Francie."

"And you can call your brother."

"Yeah, but he'd probably kill me."

"I might, too."

He blinked.

"Tim," she said clearly and steadily, "if I ever hear you have a gun again, you won't even know what hit you. Because I love you."

He hugged her back. "I'm sorry, Francie. I'm sorry I put you through this."

"If you have to stand up for yourself physically, go ahead."

"Oh, sure." He pulled away and smiled at Francie. "Like I'd make a dent on Marty Simpson."

"Ask your brother to teach you. He had trouble, but the bullies who picked on him didn't get away unscarred. Now," her voice became brisk, "go to school, and I'll get rid of the gun."

"But, Francie, you're on parole. You can't—"

She waved his objections off. "You go on. I'll take care of this."

Francie took a bus down to Town Lake. For a few minutes, she watched the joggers and followed the older couples strolling along until she reached a bridge. She walked to the middle of it and waited until she was alone. Looking down at the water, she made sure there were no fishermen or pleasure boaters below.

Finally, she opened her purse, flipped the gun out of the plastic bag and into the water. It sank under the surface immediately.

With a look around, she assured herself no one had seen her and headed back to the shore. There she dropped on to a bench and lowered her face into her hands.

She wished she knew more about praying because she really needed to pray now, big-time, but she had so little experience. She remembered how the minister had started last Sunday and whispered, *"Dear Lord,"* but stopped. What next? Uncertain, she started talking. *"Oh, Lord,"* she whispered again, *"I thought life would be easier when I found You, but it's not. It's still so hard. I thought*

I'd always feel uplifted and happy, like I did at that revival, but I don't. I thought I'd grow to be strong, like the woman I sat next to, but I'm not." She shook her head. *"I thought things would be better, God. Different."*

She lifted her head and looked across the lake. *"Well, God, I guess things are different. I'm not alone. I don't have to carry the burden by myself. Thank You for shouldering a lot of it."*

After a few minutes of allowing the warm breeze to blow across her face, she checked her watch. Almost noon. *"Please help Tim and thank you for listening,"* she whispered as she jumped to her feet and ran to the street where she grabbed a bus to the diner. On the way from the bus stop to the diner, she tossed the packet of bullets into a trash can in an alley.

Francie was not at all surprised to discover when she walked into the diner there was a message from Mr. Fairchild.

"Call him as soon as you can." Julie handed her a note with his number on it. "He said you missed your appointment."

She nodded.

"What happened? You in trouble?"

"Nah," Francie answered but was fairly sure she was, at least with her parole officer.

"Something I had to take care of with Tim." She looked at Julie. "How are you doing? Get some sleep? Feeling better?"

"I was fine when I came in, but now I'm running my feet off to take care of all the customers by myself."

Francie took the hint and headed toward the back to wash her hands.

When she finished and passed by the stove, Manny said, "You look terrible, Francie. Everything okay? Did you get whatever it was taken care of?"

"Yes, it's okay. I hope." Then she moved toward the booth Julie pointed to and began to take orders.

It was almost two before Miss Calhoun called him. By that time, Brandon was getting more worried wondering where she was. He had been distracted with his other parolees, not the professional behavior he prided himself on.

It wasn't like her to miss class, then to leave work and miss an appointment. At least, he *thought* this wasn't like her.

No one at the diner had known where she'd gone. Manny said she'd just left. She hadn't called him to tell him she'd miss the appointment. Of course, she had no phone in her apartment. He had the number for the neighbor down the hall. He'd try her if Miss Calhoun didn't call soon.

Could she have gone home to bed, not feeling well?

Maybe she'd been hit by a car on the way to their appointment. Should he call the hospitals?

All that worrying was the reason he was so angry when she finally did call. "Where were you?" he demanded. "You missed your appointment."

"Yes, I did, and I'm sorry. I'd like to reschedule. Would later this afternoon be okay?"

"No." He didn't want to see her this afternoon. He knew his anger would take over. Even now he had to struggle to remain calm.

But he had to see her. As her parole officer, it was important that he see her. "I mean, yes. I have an opening at three-thirty."

"All right. I'll be there. Thank you for making time for me."

At three-twenty, Brandon was completing his appointment with another parolee but he had difficulty concentrating.

What had gotten into him? He took it for granted his parolees would miss appointments, often without any explanation other than, "I forgot." Often they added a glare, a dare for him to push them, but usually they really had forgotten and didn't care.

He'd thought Miss Calhoun was better than the others. She was going to school and church and had shown herself reliable—until recently.

What was wrong with him? Why should he think she was better than his other clients? Parolees were ex-cons. Ex-cons had just gotten out of prison. By definition, they couldn't be trusted or they wouldn't have been in prison to start with.

The problem was obvious: he was having a hard time remembering Miss Calhoun was an ex-con, that she'd been in prison. His attitude toward her concerned him a lot. Being as upset as he was about her not keeping an appointment infuriated him even more.

Even his relief that she hadn't been hurt didn't calm him much.

Until she walked into the reception area. All the sparkle was gone from her eyes. Her cheeks were pale. Even her hair didn't look springy.

What had happened to her?

In an instant, his anger evaporated. What he wanted to do was hug her and comfort her and tell her everything—even whatever it was that had drained all the life and joy from her—would be all right.

He shook himself. Of course he couldn't do that. He was her parole officer. He was a professional, but he wasn't acting like one. He should lecture her harshly for missing the appointment and not calling.

Besides, since he didn't know what had upset her, he could hardly promise she'd be okay. False hope. He couldn't believe he'd wanted to offer it.

"Mr. Fairchild?" Petey Malloy asked in his odd falsetto voice.

He looked over the desk at Petey on the other side of his desk. He'd forgotten the man was there. He'd been so taken up with Miss Calhoun, he'd forgotten Petey. How unprofessional was that?

"That's all, Mr. Malloy." Brandon stood. "I'll see you at your job next week."

"Thank you."

Once Petey had moved away from Brandon's desk, Brandon stood and called, "Miss Calhoun?"

She got to her feet and moved slowly toward his desk. "I'm sorry I missed the earlier appointment," she said as she settled into the chair.

The Path To Love

"Are you sick, Miss Calhoun? When I called, I was told that your boss has been ill."

Scrutinizing her dejected posture, he said, "Would you like a cup of coffee?" Where had that come from? Since when was he serving refreshments.

"No, thank you. I feel fine." She forced a smile so pitiful it caused Brandon's heart to contract.

As he sat, he reminded himself he was her parole officer. Structure and firmness.

What would he say to another parolee, any other parolee? He needed to say that to her.

"Miss Calhoun, where were you this morning? Do you have a reason for missing our appointment?"

"I overslept."

"Miss Calhoun, I know that isn't true. You worked the breakfast shift this morning. Manny told me you were there. He didn't want to tell me, but he was worried. He said you left suddenly at about—" he paused to check his notes "—nine o'clock. He said he didn't know where you went."

She watched him for a long moment. "I'm sorry I lied, but I can't tell you where I was." She shook her head.

"Miss Calhoun, may I remind you that you

are on parole and that I need to know these things?" He glared at her. "Now, where were you this morning?"

She shook her head again. "I can't tell you. If you have to send me back to prison, go ahead, but it can't tell you. It's not mine to tell."

"Are you protecting someone?" What a dumb question. Of course she was.

She refused to meet his eyes.

What was he going to do? The amazing thing was he really didn't know. He'd completely lost any objectivity. Whereas he should be reading the riot act to her, he felt that he couldn't add to her worries.

So he said, "All right, Miss Calhoun. I'll give you one more chance." He opened her file and started to make a note before he added, "Only this one, but you're still on thin ice with me."

"Thank you. I really appreciate it and I promise I won't miss anything again."

He glanced up to find her leaning back in her chair, looking exhausted. "You promised me that last week, Miss Calhoun. You do realize that keeping up with your parole officer is the most important part of your life now. Remember, I can have your parole revoked if you are not honest with me, if you miss an appointment, a class or work."

"Yes, sir. Thank you. For not doing that this time."

"Now, why don't you tell me about the last two weeks, your job and school, anything you need to."

He listened as she spoke. Little by little, color returned to her face and her eyes gained a little warmth and enthusiasm. It must be hard to keep Francie Calhoun down. An admirable trait, but he still wished he knew what had troubled her in the first place.

By three-fifty, he'd finished questioning her. She left, still not the Francie—Miss Calhoun—he was used to seeing but, at least, she wasn't quite as upset as when she'd entered.

The pleasure her recovery gave him caused warning bells to go off. Together with the warmth and delight her presence gave him, it caused him to stare at the door long after Miss Calhoun had left.

What was happening to him?

He'd lost all objectivity with this parolee. He wanted to believe every word she said, a serious mistake with a parolee. He even wanted to comfort he when she was sad. How did he know she wasn't conning him? All those thoughts crowding into his brain set off an additional warning. Maybe he needed to talk to his supervisor because he wasn't at all sure if he could work with Miss Calhoun any longer.

After work that day, Brandon met his brother-in-law Phil Jurenka for a game of racquetball at a neighborhood racket club.

"You're not on your game," Phil said as they toweled off between serves. "I'm beating you more easily than usual."

"The day an old man with two children and another on the way can beat me, I'll quit." Brandon tossed his towel on the bench as went back on the court.

"Then you'd better get ready to retire," Phil said. "Because I'm going to beat you, brother."

What was wrong with him? He didn't have the usual power in his serve and was slow on the return. Not only that, but he wasn't catching sight of the ball as early as he usually did. The last one had almost hit him in the face before he'd throw the racket up to protect himself.

After finally pulling out a narrow win, Brandon headed for the shower while Phil tossed his equipment in a bag and headed home. While the water streamed down his face,

Brandon had to admit that the problem with his racquetball game and everything else was his unprofessional interest in Miss Calhoun.

Tomorrow he'd make an appointment with Maxine Kaplan, his supervisor, to explain the situation.

"Does Miss Calhoun know of your interest?" Maxine asked.

"I'm sure she doesn't. I've never said a word that wasn't professional, but I'm more interested in her as a woman than I should be."

Maxine nodded. "Knowing you, Brandon, I'm sure you've acted honorably. I'll transfer Miss Calhoun to another parole officer.

"A good one," Brandon said. "Not another Gentry."

"I hope we don't have any more Gentries, but I'll make sure she has one as good as you. Well, almost as good as you."

Chapter Six

"Francie, order up." Manny placed two huge platters filled with eggs, sausage, hash browns, grits and a side of toast on the counter.

It had been a fairly easy two weeks. Cops had come into the diner but only to eat, not to pass along any information about Tim, which was a great relief.

She'd finished her finals and done well. After a week of rest, she'd start fall semester, taking Spanish—which Manny said he'd help her with—American history and college algebra. The math course scared her to death.

Because the Montoyas hadn't called, she guessed there were no problems with Tim. Of course, Tim hadn't called to tell her life was cool. Not that she'd thought he would. He was, after all, a teenage boy. A very embarrassed teenage boy.

Mike had been in the diner the day before, overflowing with enthusiasm. He'd just started medical school. It was great and so was Cynthia.

Picking up the plates and balancing them on her left arm while she grabbed a coffeepot, Francie served her table and filled their cups.

"Thanks, Francie." Gus Brewer smiled up at her. "You're looking pretty today."

"Oh, Gus, stop trying to flirt with Francie. She's much too young for you," his wife said.

Enjoying the banter and friendship of her regulars, Francie grinned at them both.

She hadn't missed a day of work or school, not a Sunday at church. The minister had greeted her by name the week before and invited her to a Sunday-school class.

"I don't know, Reverend Miller. It would be embarrassing for me to be with all these people who knew the Bible. I'm so new at all this."

"Francie, this is a class for new Christians. You're all at the same place."

She considered it for a moment before agreeing. "I'll never learn anything if I don't try. I'll be there."

How amazing. She was going to be in a

Sunday-school class. She couldn't wait to tell Mr. Fairchild about that the next time she saw him.

Oh, yes, she knew very well she shouldn't look forward to seeing her parole officer. She shouldn't even think about him between appointments. She'd never thought about Mr. Gentry from month to month. Of course, Mr. Gentry had never looked like Mr. Fairchild and was thirty years older than her and wiped his nose with the back of his hand. No one could have looked forward to seeing Mr. Gentry.

Picking up the coffeepot again, Francie wandered through the diner filling cups.

Last week, she'd visited the financial-assistance office and thought the chances were good she'd get help with tuition and books. Maybe she could start saving money. Maybe she could get some health insurance. Maybe she could even afford to get a new pair of shoes.

On top of that, she had an appointment with the vocational counselor in two weeks. Altogether, life had improved greatly.

She could hardly wait to tell Mr. Fairchild all of this—except she'd promised herself not to think of her parole officer between appointments.

The only cloud came in the form of Manny and Julie—a pretty big problem to ignore. Francie had caught Manny watching Julie, who still wasn't feeling terrific. Over and over, he told her to go home and rest until she was well, but Julie refused to listen to him. They didn't fight openly, odd for both of those strong-willed, hot-tempered people. In fact, they were usually coolly polite to each other. On top of that, they didn't want to talk to her about the situation between the two of them. They refused to believe there *was* a situation.

Besides, the tension between two of her favorite people was none of her business. Her business was keeping herself clean and straight, supporting herself and going to school and church.

All that was more than enough to keep her busy. She did not have to take on Julie's and Manny's troubles, but she couldn't talk herself out of worrying about them, couldn't help wishing they got along better.

Francie glanced around the almost empty diner then up at the clock. Last week, someone had called the diner and left a message changing her appointment to this afternoon. No reason had been given, but it worked okay.

"Julie, I need to leave now."

"Okay, Francie. See you tomorrow."

Thanks to the man who had taken ten minutes to decide on his lunch order, she was running a little behind again. She didn't change clothes, but pulled her sweater over her uniform.

By running from the bus stop to the parole office once more, she arrived at the office only a few minutes late and panting. With a few pats to her hair, she rushed inside.

There was still a parolee in Mr. Fairchild's cubicle. Good. She hadn't kept him waiting.

After Francie took a few deep breaths and checked in, the receptionist said, "Miss Calhoun, Mrs. Rivera is running a few minutes behind. She'll be with you shortly."

"Mrs. Rivera? That must be a mistake. Mr. Fairchild is my parole officer," Francie explained.

"I don't believe so." The receptionist looked at the appointment schedule on her monitor. "No, you've been switched to Mrs. Rivera."

Francie stumbled back to the wooden chair and looked into Mr. Fairchild's cubicle. What had happened?

The intercom on the receptionist's desk buzzed. After listening for a moment, she said, "Mrs. Rivera's ready for you now. Her cubicle is at the end on the left."

In a fog, Francie stood. She looked at Mr. Fairchild again. He looked up at her for less than a second but dropped his gaze before they made eye contact.

"Hello, Miss Calhoun." Mrs. Rivera, a tall, dark Latina women with a trace of accent, stood and motioned Francie toward the chair.

"Mrs. Rivera," Francie said as she sat.

"I've been looking over your file, Miss Calhoun. I'm pleased to see you're in school and employed. Why don't you tell me about yourself."

Francie answered a few questions before she said, "Mrs. Rivera, I'm sure you're a wonderful parole officer, but Mr. Fairchild has been very helpful. I don't know why I was transferred to you. I wondered if I could be reassigned to him."

"No, Miss Calhoun, that wouldn't be possible. This was not an overload situation. Mr. Fairchild himself requested the change."

She sat back, stunned. What had she done wrong? Why had he requested the change? She thought they'd gotten along well. He'd helped her so much, encouraged her to go to church and to read the Bible. He'd shown interest in her life and problems. Because of him, she'd have financial aid and vocational counseling.

Not only that, but she'd miss him.

Startled, she blinked as she considered the thought. He was her parole officer. She should be grateful for what he'd done but this shouldn't be a personal thing. She shouldn't miss him, as handsome as he was.

Uh-oh. That was another thought she shouldn't have. He was her parole officers, not some movie star.

Besides, probably Mrs. Rivera would be as supportive. She seemed nice enough, interested in Francie and her future.

But she wasn't Mr. Fairchild.

After ten minutes, Mrs. Rivera said, "I believe that's all, Miss Calhoun. Mr. Fairchild has kept your information up-to-date. According to his notes, you prefer morning appointments." She looked at her calendar. "I have ten-thirty for three weeks from today open."

Francie nodded. "That's fine." She stood and pulled her sweater more tightly around her.

When she got to the reception area, she saw Mr. Fairchild's client leaving. Without a thought, she hurried into his cubicle and sat down.

* * *

Brandon was glad Sean had arrived a little early for his appointment. The young man had just settled in Brandon's office when Miss Calhoun entered the reception area. She looked like sunshine in her yellow uniform and with the energy that radiated from her. In spite of everything she'd gone through, there was so much life in her.

Because her cheeks were red and her hair out of control, he guessed she'd been running. He almost smiled at the picture until realized Sean was waiting for him to answer a question.

Brandon knew Olga, the receptionist, would tell Miss Calhoun about the change in parole officers. He didn't want to see Francie's reaction, but he couldn't completely ignore it. For a moment, he looked up. The impression of enormous blue eyes and a face pale with shock bothered him as he looked quickly back at Sean's file. Should he have told her himself? How would he have done that? What would he have said? That he couldn't work with her anymore because he found her too attractive? Not something he'd ever thought he'd feel. Certainly nothing a parole officer should confess to his client.

No, even telling her about the transfer would have been unprofessional. This was the best solution. He wouldn't have to see her again, wouldn't have to worry that his interest in her would make her uncomfortable. Anita was a great parole officer. She'd do a good job with Miss Calhoun.

"Mr. Fairchild?" Sean said. "Are you all right?"

He concentrated on Sean's problems and myriad of questions concerning everything in his life.

Unfortunately, just as he and Sean finished and Sean headed toward the door, Miss Calhoun walked across the floor of the reception room to leave. For a second, she stopped and looked at him, then moved quickly toward his desk, nimbly dodging Sean. Before Brandon could do or say anything, she slipped into the chair Sean had vacated.

She watched him for almost a minute before she said, "I know I probably shouldn't do this, but I've always discovered that if I want to know something, it works out best if I ask." She paused. "Why did you have another parole officer take over my case?"

"This isn't something I can discuss with you here, Miss Calhoun."

"I mean, I thought we got along well. You've helped me a great deal. Didn't you think I was doing well? Were you angry because I missed the last appointment?"

"No, of course I wasn't. Well, I was for a while but that wasn't the reason I asked for the change."

She leaned forward. He'd forgotten the emotion her eyes could convey: abandonment, pain, bewilderment. Each made him feel incredibly guilty. Every one of them was an emotion he shouldn't have caused a parolee who was trying as hard to rehabilitate herself as Miss Calhoun.

And none of these were reactions his having her case transferred should have aroused in a parolee.

When she didn't say anything, Brandon repeated, "That wasn't the reason I asked for the change."

"Then why? Was your caseload too heavy?"

"It always is, but that wasn't the reason."

"Then it was me, right? I did something wrong?"

"Miss Calhoun, I can't tell you here. If you like, I'll drop by the diner and explain." She deserved that. He couldn't allow her to think she was responsible, that she'd failed somehow.

Why hadn't he realized she'd leap to that conclusion? As embarrassing as an explanation would be, she needed to know the transfer was because he couldn't work with her anymore.

"Yes, please."

"This was not your fault. Please believe me." He stood.

She got to her feet but didn't look convinced. "All right. Thank you. I'll look forward to seeing you."

Finding the time to go to the diner wasn't difficult for Brandon. Finding the courage was. It took him nearly a week before he dropped in at the diner. He'd even changed his schedule that day so he'd arrive at two in the afternoon, hoping Miss Calhoun would have already left.

Not that there was anything wrong about having her case transferred to Anita Rivera. Anita was a very good parole officer. As soon as he'd realized his attraction to Francie—Miss Calhoun—he'd acted professionally, stepping away.

No, not exactly right. He'd recognized the chemistry from the beginning and had attempted to deal with it. He had done nothing unethical. He'd made sure he'd done all the background work, the home and work visits, and the follow-ups with other agencies.

He'd been a much better parole officer than Gentry but that was like saying he'd been a better parole officer than, oh, the three Stooges or Bugs Bunny. Even a red brick would have been better than Gentry.

Now what?

It was two-fifteen. He still stood outside the diner, feeling as if his feet were attached to the concrete. Of course he felt guilty. He should have explained earlier.

Would seeing her today make anything better?

If he moved a little closer to the door, he could look inside to see if Miss Calhoun were there. Of course, if he moved a little closer, anyone inside could see him. He'd look like an idiot, peering through the window but not going inside.

"Are you coming inside or not, Fairchild?"

He looked up to see Julie standing a few feet away, just on the other side of the door.

"Francie's fixin' to leave if you aren't coming in." She glared at him. "She tried to escape out the alley door to dodge you, but I stopped her. Told her she was a coward and had to face you."

Escaping through the back door. A morti-fying but efficient tactic to avoid him. Obvi-ously she didn't want to see him, either.

Brandon walked through the door Julie held open. Miss Calhoun stood against the counter looking as embarrassed as he felt.

"Good afternoon, Miss Calhoun." He nod-ded at her.

"Mr. Fairchild." She nodded back.

"I wonder if I might have a cup of coffee and the pleasure of your company for a few minutes?" He sounded like the hero of an old British movie. Right now he was glad he at least had that example because words were not exactly flowing from his mouth.

"Of course." Miss Calhoun filled a mug, grabbed a handful of creamers, and moved toward the booth Brandon had chosen.

When she put the cup and creamers down but continued to stand, he said, "Please join me?"

She paused before sliding into the bench across from him and lifting her eyes to his. Her fingers drummed a soft beat on the table.

"I wanted to explain the reason I re-quested to have you transferred to another parole officer."

She nodded again but didn't say anything,

dropping her gaze to her tapping fingers. She wasn't going to make this easy. She wasn't going to look at him until he said something to explain why he'd had her transferred. He cleared his throat because words didn't come.

"Miss Calhoun." Brandon reached out and took her hand to stop the sound.

She looked up at him while trying to pull her hand away but he didn't let go.

He nodded at their clasped hands. "That's the reason I asked Mrs. Rivera to take over. That's exactly why."

When she titled her head in confusion, he added, "I told my supervisor that I find you far too attractive to be objective about your rehabilitation."

"What?" Her glance shot up to his face. "You find me attractive? That's crazy." She gestured toward herself with the hand he wasn't holding. "Why?"

He laughed uncomfortably. "I don't know, exactly."

She didn't look happy with his confession, and he had to agree with her judgment. It wasn't the most flattering thing to say.

"You can't tell me I'm the first man who has found you attractive."

"Pretty much." Miss Calhoun nodded. "I

didn't have much time to date in high school. They don't have proms in juvie, and it's hard to meet guys in prison, so I don't have a lot of experience in this area."

"Then, well, yes, I do find you attractive. You're going to have to trust me about that."

"I don't do trust very well,' she mumbled before his words sunk in. Then her eyes filled with wonder. "Really? You really do? Find *me* attractive?"

"Yes." Now he could smile a little. "You are a lovely young woman, and I admire you greatly for what you are doing to pull your life together."

She titled her head, a little puzzled. "Thank you, Mr. Fairchild. That's very nice, but why did you bother to come here to tell me that?"

"I saw how hurt you were when Olga told you that you had a new parole officer, as if I'd betrayed you. I wanted to explain the problem isn't you. It's me. I realized I couldn't be objective with a client I find attractive."

She nodded and thought. "I appreciate your honesty. Thank you." She started to slide out of the booth, but he didn't let go of her hand.

"Is there any more you need to say?" She glanced from their hands to his eyes.

He released his grip on her hand to hold it more gently. "I'd like to spend time with you." He stopped and looked deeply into her eyes. "To get to know you."

"Oh." She considered for a moment. "That would be nice," she whispered before looking around the diner. He followed her gaze.

Manny was pretending to put orders up, but, since there were no customers in the place, he was actually watching them. So was Julie, who had already wiped down all the tables three or four times but was concentrating fiercely on the ones closest to them. She was pressing down so hard Francie feared her boss would wipe the beige design off the tops.

Brandon reached in his pocket and tossed a couple of bills on the table. "What are you doing now? Would you like to take a walk, maybe talk a little? I've missed seeing you."

"She's got a Spanish quiz tomorrow," Julie shouted. "She works hard and needs to sleep and study. Don't take up too much of her time."

"Stay out of this, Julie," Manny said. "They're adults and don't need you telling them what to do and what not to do." He looked at the two in the booth and said, "Have fun, kids. See you tomorrow, Francie."

Brandon couldn't help smiling. "Would you like to take a walk, Miss Calhoun?"

"Oh, for goodness's sake, if you came here to tell her you're attracted to her, surely you can call her Francie." Julie said.

"Francie, would you take a walk with me?" He watched her, trying to read her expression.

"That would be very nice, Mr. Fairchild."

"Maybe you could call me Brandon." He stopped for a minute, stricken. "Do you find me at all attractive? Do you share some of my feelings or am I assuming that you do? I mean, you've never said anything. You've never showed me that you even liked me."

"I have to tell you—" Francie began as she struggled to sit up straight on the lumpy seat of the booth. With an eye on Julie, she whispered, "I have to tell you I do think you're very handsome and so nice to care about me by setting up all those appointments for me."

"That was part of my job, Miss…I mean, Francie, but *nice* wasn't the response I was looking for. *Handsome* is a good start."

She nodded.

"Have you ever considered whether we could see each other outside of the professional relationship we used to have?"

She wiggled again. "No, I haven't."

He was making her uncomfortable. Maybe he'd done all this—been nervous and worried and forced himself to come in and talk with her—when the feelings were one-sided. Maybe she didn't care about him at all.

After all, the scene in his office when she'd wanted to know why he'd transferred her to another parole officer might not have been because she felt something for him. It could have been because he'd been a good parole officer, and she didn't understand why he'd gotten rid of her.

Where did he get off thinking he was the answer to every woman's prayers?

Well, he'd never thought he was before, but he hoped Francie liked him, at least a little. At least enough for them to get to know each other.

"Would you like to?" he asked.

She hadn't pulled her hand out of his. That was a good sign. Surely she'd have done that earlier if she weren't comfortable.

Did he want just comfortable? No, he was hoping for more, but comfortable would do as a start. They could work from there.

Why didn't she say anything?

"Miss Calhoun?" he prompted. "Francie?"

"I don't know. I'd never considered it."

What an idiot he'd been. He put her hand down and started to slide out of the booth.

"Mr. Fair... I mean, Brandon...like I said, I find you attractive." She put her hand over his to stop him. "How could I not? But this is such a surprise." She leaned toward him. "I never thought that you...that I...that we could, you know, ever have the opportunity to get to know each other. That you'd want to get to know one of your clients outside the office."

He could understand that. They were not the usual couple.

"I mean, you and I are an odd combination." She smiled at him.

"True, but that doesn't mean we couldn't see each other, does it?"

"Oh, for goodness's sakes, Francie, give the guy a break," Julie shouted. "You've been telling me what a hunk he is for weeks. Don't pass up this opportunity."

"Leave them alone," Manny told Julie. "They can handle this without your interference."

"Yes, I'd like to take a walk." Francie slid out of the booth and headed toward the door as she waved toward her boss. "Thanks for all the help, Julie. I'll take it from here."

Chapter Seven

"How'd yesterday go?"

Francie looked up at Julie who had slid into the booth across from her. "Fine." She looked down at her notes, still a little drowsy from studying late. "I got a lot done."

"Well, if you don't want to tell me the details…" Julie moved back across the seat to stand.

"Details about what?" She shook her head. "I spent most of the evening conjugating Spanish verbs."

"I'm not asking about how you studied for the test." Julie rolled her eyes. "I want to know about you and the hunk, Mr. Fairchild."

"Oh, that." Francie grimaced.

"Yes, that. How could you forget?"

"Not much happened." She closed the book and stretched. "We walked and chatted for a few minutes, then he had to run off for an appointment. That was it."

"That was it?" Julie fell back against the cushion. "He didn't ask you out?"

Francie shook her head.

"Then why did the man bother to come down and see you? Why did he tell you he found you attractive if he wasn't going to do something about it?"

"I guess he came down to explain why he wasn't my parole officer anymore. I think you and I read more into what happened, you know, him coming down here, than there was." She shrugged. "Besides, Julie, we're such different people. He's educated and has a good job."

"Not *that* good a job. I bet he doesn't take home fifty thousand, if that much."

"Sounds like a great job to me. As you know, I don't make quite that much."

"Francie, I'm sorry. You know if I could afford more, I'd give you a raise."

"Julie, I'm not complaining, just comparing. You pay me more than most waitresses earn, and I was really desperate and inexperienced when I started here. I'll always appreciate that.

And I'll never forget how you took a chance on me when no one else would hire me."

Julie looked down and fiddled with the handle of her cup. "Like I said, it wasn't a big deal."

"But it was, Julie." She paused and added, "Why did you do it? I've always wondered why you risked hiring me."

"I thought you looked like you had determination, and, besides…" She took a long drink of her coffee.

"And besides?" Francie prompted.

"All right." She leaned back in the booth and took a deep breath. "I was desperate, too. I really needed help. The waitress before you left without giving notice, and I was working all three meals. I hired you because you were the only one who applied."

"Oh." Francie thought for a minute before she laughed and put her hand over Julie's. "That's okay. I don't really care why you hired me. I'm still thankful."

"Well, anyway, getting back to the important stuff, I think you and your parole officer make a cute couple," Julie said.

"Oh, sure. He dresses well and seems so sure of himself. Then there's me, Francie Calhoun. I have more arrests than I have

T-shirts and have to work constantly to patch up my confidence."

"So what? I thought he was able to see past that. He said he could. He thinks you're tough and hard-working."

"Those are qualities that really interest a man."

"You're real pretty, too," Manny shouted.

"Yes, you're real pretty, too," Julie repeated. "Mr. Fairchild told you he finds you attractive, and you're working hard to change your life and be a good example for your cousins. He's got to admire you."

"Thanks, Julie. I appreciate that, but it may not be enough for Mr. Fairchild. If it isn't," Francie said with a shrug, "well, I don't have any more to offer. Besides, in spite of all he said in here, remember, he didn't ask me out when we left here."

"What did you do?"

"We walked for a few blocks and talked, then he had to leave for an appointment. Just left."

"If he did that, forget about the bum," Manny said.

"That won't be hard if I don't see him again." She opened the book. "I've got to study, Julie. That history test is tomorrow afternoon."

"Don't know why you study so much. I bet you get an A. You always do."

"I get As because I study," Francie looked down at the text.

"Well, yes, but why so much? You always do well."

"Because I'm afraid I'll forget. I didn't use my brain for so long I have to work really hard." She glanced at Julie. "I'm afraid if I don't have the information deep in my brain, almost engraved on it, it'll just fly off into space." With a smile, she flipped her book open and immersed herself in the Battle of Saratoga.

Trying to figure out what he was going to do about Francie Calhoun wasn't easy.

Brandon sat in his car in front of his parents' house, the big barn he'd grown up in, drumming his fingers on the steering wheel and thinking. While Francie had been shuffled from home to home and family to family, he'd been raised in a lovely house, large and comfortable, filled with *his* family.

After a check of his watch, he realized he'd have to go inside the house in a minute. His family was gathering for dinner, but this seemed like the only waking minute he'd had to himself for a week. Or maybe he hadn't found time because he didn't want to consider if he'd made a mistake, if he was going to hurt the feelings of a young woman who didn't deserve that.

Could there ever be anything between two such different people?

"Are you still driving this old clunker? Why are you just parked there? Come on in."

Recognizing the voice of his sister Miriam, Brandon grinned and glanced up to see her looking in his window. "Yes, and trying to gather up my courage to face the crowd inside."

She pulled open the car door and grabbed his hand to drag her brother out. "What crowd? It's just Mom and Dad and me and Phil and the kids—oh, and Susanne and her newest boyfriend."

"Sounds intimidating to me." He stood and hugged her, unable to get his arms around her. "Actually, you're kind of a crowd all by yourself."

"Never make fun of a pregnant woman. You never know how her hormones will react."

"I thought you were a strong, responsible woman who never blamed anything on hormones."

"That's when I'm not pregnant."

Tugging his arm, she dragged Brandon toward the house. "I do wish you and our sister would get married," she grinned, "Not to each other, of course. Providing Mom and Dad with their grandchildren should not be a one-woman job." She leaned on his arm for balance as they went up the broad steps to the wide front porch.

"As long as you're producing them so well, I'm going to leave it up to you."

She stopped on the porch and turned toward Brandon. "Haven't you found a nice woman to marry yet?"

Had he? No, how could he have? He looked at his sister and wondered how he could expose her young children to an ex-con. He glanced up at white pillars and the beautiful Georgian facade of the house and realized how out-of-place Francie would be, how out-of-place she would feel here.

"Brandon, have you met someone?"

Bah. He should have remembered that Miriam could always read his expression. "Of course not. You know I'd tell you."

Then his mother, tall and graceful in lovely salmon-colored silk slacks and a matching shirt, came out of the house.

"Brandon." She enfolded him in a hug. "It's been weeks since you've been by." Taking his hand, she said, "Come inside. Your father has Susanne's young man cornered and is grilling him about where he goes to church. I don't think this Peter is ready for your father yet."

They joined his father, his sister Susanne, and her date Peter in the family room, the least formal room in the house. It was three times the size of Francie's apartment and glowed in the light of an enormous wooden chandelier. Two comfortable couches upholstered in green-and-blue plaid faced each other. The contrast between this room and Francie's tiny apartment astounded him.

With the difference in their backgrounds and lives, how could he ever have thought there could be anything between him and Francie?

And yet, later that evening, while his mother and father sat on one sofa, Phil had his arm around Miriam on the other with their son and daughter on their laps, and Susanne laughed up at Peter, Brandon realized how alone he was. Odd, he'd never felt like that before with his family.

"Tell us about your work, Brandon," his mother urged.

When he finished, Phil and Miriam asked for ideas on the thrift shop they were setting up in the community. Flighty Susanne had told about the literacy classes she taught at church, hours of volunteer work on top of her busy schedule as a lawyer.

"We are so proud of you children," their father said. "We hoped your would show your Christian faith through service to all of God's children."

Yes, Robert and Hilda Fairchild had always expected their children to witness, but they'd been wonderful examples with all they did for others.

Wasn't Francie one of God's children? Well, of course she was. How arrogant of him to question that.

So how could he witness to her?

A few days later, Francie was wiping down the last tables as the lunch crowd thinned out. Hearing the door open, she cringed. She'd thought they had finished serving, had hoped she could take a walk while it was still warm enough to stroll along without a coat. She had a vision of stopping in a park to sit on the bench and read her Bible.

Or maybe she could go home, take her shoes off and curl up on the couch for a nap.

But the door slid shut as a customer entered. Forcing back a sigh, Francie turned toward him and could only be happy she wasn't holding a pitcher again.

It was Mr. Fairchild. Why was he here?

After waiting for him to show up, looking for him for days whenever the door opened, she'd given up expecting to see him. It had hurt because she'd trusted him, believed he really wanted to see her again—then nothing. Now she didn't want to see him again, didn't want to start hoping again.

She looked around for Julie to take his table, but her boss had headed into the kitchen with a bin of dirty glasses for Harold the dishwasher to finish up. Besides, it would be immature and not at all kind or generous to ignore him. And Julie would be very angry if Francie didn't immediately welcome a customer. After all, it was Julie's business, and Julie paid her to wait on customers, every customer.

"Hello, Mr. Fairchild," she said. "Do you prefer a booth or a table?"

He raised an eyebrow in that really classy way he had. "Mr. Fairchild? I thought we'd moved past that, Francie."

Because she'd look petty if she kept acting so…well, petty, she smiled. "Here's a nice table over here. I'll get you some coffee."

He reached his hand out to stop her. "No, I'll have iced tea, sweetened please, and a bowl of whatever soup your cook has made for today."

When she returned with the tea and soup, he said, "Can you join me for a minute?"

She couldn't lie. It was obvious she had nothing else to do. There was only one other filled table, and the people there were chatting while they finished the coffee Francie had just poured for them. The other tables were empty and clean.

If only Julie and Manny weren't watching from the kitchen, attempting to look busy. Julie even waved her hands to tell Francie to sit down. She bet Julie thought they were being inconspicuous, but Francie didn't miss the signal and neither did Mr. Fairchild—Brandon.

"Yes, that would be nice." Francie pulled a chair out and settled in it.

How was she supposed to behave with this man who had said she was attractive, who had told he wanted to get to know her better, but didn't do anything about it? How should she react sitting across the table from a man who had her transferred to another parole officer because he couldn't work with a client for whom he had unprofessional feelings?

"How has your week gone?" he asked after a few minutes of silence.

"Fine." She stopped herself from playing with the paper napkin when she realized she'd torn a strip off it. "And yours?"

"Fine." He took another spoonful of soup. "This is great soup," he added after another minute without a word.

Other than their contact through the legal system, they had nothing in common. *Nothing,* she repeated to herself.

"How's church?"

"I'm still going to the one I told you about. One of the ladies on the evangelism committee gave me a pot of flowers last week. They look really pretty in the apartment." She smiled at the memory of the spot of red on the table and the delight the generous gift had brought her. "And the minister said he'd wanted to call me, but they didn't have my phone number."

"That's good. Sounds like a nice place." Brandon finished the soup and pushed the bowl aside.

"I told him I'm an ex-con, but that didn't

upset him. He said they're glad I'd found their church." She shook her head. "Wasn't that nice? I didn't expect that."

"I told you the right church would welcome you."

When Francie started to say something else, she noticed that the customers at the other table were finished.

"Excuse me." Francie stood to clear it off but was almost run over by Julie who had dashed out of the kitchen.

"Sit down, Francie. I'll take care of them," Julie said.

"Go ahead with your work, Francie," Brandon said. "I have to get back to work. I'm visiting a job site on the way. Since I was close, I thought I'd stop in." He stood, threw a couple of bills on the table and looked down at Francie for a few seconds. Then he seemed to rouse himself as he turned toward the door and left.

"When is that man going to do something about the way he feels about you?" Julie shook her head.

"Oh, I don't think he feels a thing." Francie picked up his glass and bowl. "He comes here because he likes Manny's cooking."

Julie shook her head again. "I saw it, the

way he looks at you. Very soft, very gentle. He's interested in you, but he doesn't know what to do about it."

"Oh, sure." Francie went around her boss and toward the bin for dirty dishes.

"Even Manny noticed it," Julie said. "Didn't you, Manny?"

"Yeah," Manny agreed while he cleaned the grill. "Even *I* noticed it."

"Well, Mr. Fairchild's not doing much about it, so it doesn't make much difference, does it?" Francie started back toward the table with a sponge.

"And, Julie—" she turned toward her friend "—don't you do or say a thing, not one thing, about it." She glared at Julie. "Don't you ask him how he feels or why he hasn't asked me out. That would embarrass me to death. Besides, this is my life and I can handle it."

Julie nodded. "Okay, Francie."

Francie didn't believe her for a minute.

"You know she's going to, Francie," Manny warned. "When Mr. Fairchild comes here again, she's going to sit down with him like she did before, ask him why he hasn't asked you out. If you don't want her to barrel into your life, you'd better do something yourself, before she does." He shook his head. "You know how stubborn she is."

"Me, stubborn?" Julie turned her attention to Manny. "What do you mean?"

Francie left them to their argument, thankful for a few minutes that their attention was no longer focused on her.

But she knew Manny was right.

Almost a week passed. With every day, Francie worried. Would he come? Would Mr. Fairchild—Brandon—stop in again for lunch, making her wonder why he was there? Making her nervous because she could feel the pull of attraction between the two of them. If he did, would Julie say something to mortify her?

On the other hand, maybe he wouldn't come after all, a possibility which seemed even worse than the idea that Julie might embarrass her.

But he did come. Ten days after the last visit, as Francie was getting her things together to leave a little early to work on a history paper, she ran right into him as she was leaving and almost fell down.

"I'm sorry, Francie," he said as he steadied her with an arm.

She looked back at Julie and Manny. Her boss was grinning slyly; the cook was shaking his head and pointing at Julie.

"Get out of here now, Francie!" Manny shouted.

Francie grabbed Brandon's arm and pulled him out of the diner.

Before Francie dragged him out of the diner, before he'd even entered, Brandon had stood outside the door and wondered why he hadn't come to see the woman he wanted to be with days earlier.

The only reason he could come up with was that he was a coward, afraid to reach out for something—someone—he wanted very much, scared he would be getting into a situation he couldn't control.

Fortunately, he didn't have to say a word or do anything because Francie took charge.

She'd grabbed his hand and pulled him after her, striding quickly and full of purpose past the few other pedestrians on the sidewalk. She stopped only when they reached a small park. Well, not really a park. The area was set back from the noisy street in a narrow space left by with the destruction of an old building. When they left the street and walked the short path to the benches, Brandon was amazed that a place like this could exist in downtown Austin. There was a small fountain in the middle with four benches around it. A climbing vine left splotches of color on the brick wall of the next building.

This was a green place, with thick grass. The bushes around it added to the privacy.

"I like to come here to study and think." Francie dropped his hand and settled on a bench. "People who work around here bring their lunches and eat here, but it's pretty deserted after that."

He guessed she wanted him to follow so he did, but no sooner had he settled next to her then she leaped to her feet and started to pace around the tiny place.

He watched for almost a minute, aware of the noise of the traffic—horns, loud engines and louder music—and the smell of fumes. Ah, yes, the constant Austin traffic, intruding even in this tranquil space.

He was even more aware of her curls bouncing with each step and the thin line of her lips as she seemed to struggle with her thoughts.

"Francie?" He started to stand.

"No." She held her hand up. "Just sit there.

This is incredibly difficult for me, because I'm trying hard to think of what a Christian would do in this situation. I want to be kind and gentle and patient. Right now, I'm having a little trouble with the patient part, which isn't all that unusual."

She struggled to find words then turned toward him. "And it's hard for me to say because you've helped me so much, but I'm really confused."

"Francie?" he said again.

"I don't understand why you couldn't stay as my parole officer." She glared at him then seemed to think it over and smoothed her expression out.

He started to stand again, but she waved him back. Again.

"I told you the reason," he said. "It wasn't professional for me to work with a parolee toward whom I felt…well, an unprofessional emotion."

"You said you found me attractive." She tilted her head and watched him.

"Yes." This time he stood and went toward Francie even though she continued to move away from him. He took her hand and stilled it in a gentle grasp. "Is that a problem?"

She glanced down at the joined hands before looking up at him. "Does that happen often? That you find a woman attractive?"

"Well, it's not infrequent. Why?"

"What do you usually do when you find a woman attractive?"

He shrugged. "Often I ask them out."

She pulled her hand away. "Okay," she said. "You probably helped me more and had more interest in me than anyone in the system ever has, then you tell me you can't work with me because you can't stay professional."

He nodded and tried to hold her hand again but she put them both behind her back.

"If you usually ask other women you find attractive out, why didn't you ask *me* out?"

Well, she had him there. He should have realized she was too smart not to wonder about that, should have realized she wouldn't be in the same struggle with denial and confusion that surrounded him. Even worse, he should've realized his vacillation would hurt her.

What should he say now?

It was time for him to make up his mind.

Chapter Eight

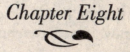

"Would you go to dinner with me?" To his surprise, the words popped out of his mouth, but they felt right.

Francie's mouth fell open. "What?"

"Didn't you ask me why I didn't ask you out?"

She nodded as she lowered herself onto the bench.

"I do want to take you out." A good start. "I admit I was very slow in getting around to it."

"Why?"

"Why was I slow?" He frowned. How could he explain that?

She nodded. "Were you—are you ashamed of me? I know we're very different, from very different backgrounds."

No, he wasn't ashamed. That wasn't the word he'd use but he could understand why she might think that. He hoped he wasn't the kind of man who would feel ashamed to be seen with anyone. Hesitant, uncertain and, probably, confused might describe how he felt, but he couldn't admit any of those feelings without hurting her.

"I didn't know if we have enough in common," he said.

She nodded again.

"But there's only one way to find out if we do or we don't. Will you go out to dinner with me?"

Francie's bewilderment showed on her face.

"Oh, excuse me." A man's voice came from the entrance to the park.

When Brandon looked over his shoulder, he saw a man with a little black dog moving away.

"You'd better agree because I'm not going to allow you to refuse." He sat next to Francie. "However, I would like to hurry this a little so we don't inconvenience people and small dogs that would like to share this place."

"Thank you, but no. I can't go to dinner with you." She sighed sadly.

"What? Why not?"

"Well, for one reason, I have nothing to wear."

He blinked. "Yes, you do." He waved toward her T-shirt, jeans and scruffy tennis shoes.

She followed his gesture and sighed again. "Oh, you're a man. You wouldn't understand. You've seen everything I have and none of it is nice enough to go to a restaurant with you, at least, not to the kind of restaurant you'd normally chose."

"Francie, I'm asking *you* out, not your clothing." He took her hand again.

"Well, thank you. That's very nice of you, but the clothes go pretty much wherever I do." She kept her eyes on their intertwined fingers. "Besides, like you said, I don't know that we have enough in common to be able to talk to each other."

"We're doing that now. Although it's about something not very important—"

She glanced up at him and frowned before dropping her gaze again.

"I'm sorry. What you wear doesn't seem important to me, but if that's important to you, I'll try to be more sympathetic." He paused. "I think the only way to find out if we have something to talk about is by going out, by getting to know each other." When she didn't answer, he said, "Francie, would you look at me?"

She lifted her beautiful but uncertain eyes to his.

"I'd like to spend time with you," he said. "If that means taking walks together or sitting in the library reading while you study or grabbing a cup of coffee someplace other than the diner, that's fine."

She nodded.

"But what I would really like to do," he continued, "is take you out to dinner."

"But—"

"You don't have to worry about where. I'll take care of that. I promise not to take you anyplace you'd feel uncomfortable. Just be ready when I show up. Okay?"

She smiled, the jubilant expression that made her eyes sparkle and his heart expand until he almost couldn't breathe. But she didn't say a word until he added, "Now it's your turn to answer me, Francie."

"Yes." She nodded. "I'd like that also. Thank you. When? Tonight?"

He shook his head. "No, I have a family dinner tonight. My father's birthday."

"Tomorrow evening I have a study group."

"Commendable. Mustn't interrupt that," he

said, sounding, he knew, exactly like a parole officer. "Then Friday?"

"Oh, yes, Friday would be wonderful."

She smiled at him, that wonderful expression that filled him with joy.

Brandon continued to look down at her, still smiling, until he realized how goofy he must look. He probably should say something. "I'll pick you up at seven? Is that convenient?" He hadn't felt so awkward around a female since junior high.

"Yes, thank you. That will give me plenty of time to get ready." She stood and turned their hands so she could shake his.

For a moment they stood holding hands, until the man with the black dog returned and mumbled, "Excuse me," again before backing away.

"I'd better get back to work." Brandon pulled his hand from her grasp but continued to look down at her. "Friday at seven."

She nodded "Friday at seven," she repeated.

Francie wanted to dance all the way back to the apartment but forced herself to walk decorously, although her feet betrayed her with an occasional hop.

Brandon had asked her out. Should she go

back and tell Julie? No, not right now. For this moment, Francie wanted to hug this to herself. Brandon had asked *her* out. Her acceptance had made him happy. By forcing him to ask her out and then accepting, she'd made him happy. Was it amazing she could do that?

But what in the world would she wear?

Not going out until Friday would give her time to find something nice to wear to dinner. Actually, even her uniform was nicer than anything else she had.

Once she got back to the apartment, she counted all the tips she could spare. She'd have plenty of time later that afternoon to finish her math, so she headed over to the thrift shop run by volunteers from her church. At the shop she saw several of the women who had been so nice to her, as well as a number she hadn't met yet. Even those women smiled at her.

"I'm looking for something to wear to church." She'd considered the whole date thing and decided an outfit she could wear both Sunday mornings and to dinner would be a perfect addition to her tiny wardrobe.

A woman whose name tag said Martha— Francie couldn't remember the names of all the people who'd welcomed her at church—led her toward a rack in the middle of the room.

"Here are the dresses." Martha said. Then she pointed toward a smaller stand against the wall. "Although you might want to start over there. Those are on sale. You might find a nice bargain."

Francie found two possibilities. One was black with a nice white collar and cuffs, but it had to be two sizes too big. Her inadequate sewing skills didn't stretch to cutting that down to size. The other one was the right size in white with pale spring flowers sprinkled over it, but this was September. Even with her limited fashion sense, Francie knew it wouldn't work, either.

What a disappointment.

"Why don't we look at separates?" Martha suggested. "We have skirts over there." She pointed. "We could probably put one together with this." Pulling out a lovely light blue blouse, Martha held it up in front of Francie. "I've always thought this was pretty, but it's so small no one has been able to wear it." She considered. "I think it would fit you perfectly."

"There's a spot on the collar," Elise pointed out. "But I think I have a solution." She dashed away.

Francie touched the sleeve. The fabric was soft against her fingers, almost like silk.

"I found this collar." Elise held out a white collar edged with lace. "I can tack this on and it will cover the stain."

The collar and the shirt together cost four dollars. That was every penny she'd set aside for this. She could wear it with her jeans. It would still look better than a T-shirt. Besides, at dinner, Brandon couldn't see below the level of the table. But when he picked her up or she wore it to church, she'd still have on old jeans and ratty shoes.

"I found the perfect skirt." Elise held up a dark blue slightly flared skirt next to the shirt.

They did look nice together, but the skirt was two dollars, more than Francie could spend without cutting into her living expenses. And if she bought the skirt, there were still her terrible shoes. Comfortable but so dirty and worn. Maybe it would be better not to buy the skirt because the length—just past the knees—would show how bad the shoes really were.

"I think there are some little canvas shoes that would look nice, too." Martha picked up a pair of navy-blue flats.

They cost fifty cents. A total of six dollars

and fifty cents. She didn't have that much. Would there be tax? Probably.

Francie picked up the shirt and collar and held her four dollars out. "I'll take these."

Martha and Elise looked at each other.

"Fifty percent off for church members," Martha said.

Francie laughed. "I doubt if there are many church members who do their shopping here." No, she didn't believe that story for a minute, but how sweet of them!

"You'd be surprised," Elise said. "If you look, you can find lots of things here. I've bought some nice things for my grandchildren."

Fifty percent off would make it three dollars and twenty-five cents. She could afford that, even with tax. When she nodded, Elise picked up the shirt, threaded a needle and attached the new collar.

As Elise finished, Francie held out her bills and watched Martha ring the sale up, fold her clothes, and slip them into a plastic bag.

"Thank you," Francie said. "You are so generous. I can't tell you how much I appreciate this."

"You've brought us so much joy at church, Francie." Martha handed her the sack and change. "As I watch you learning and growing in your beliefs, you inspire me. Thank you for your faithfulness."

Francie could feel joy spreading through her. "That's the nicest thing anyone's ever said to me."

Except for Brandon telling her he found her attractive.

"If anything doesn't work, you come back and tell us," Elisa added. "And if we get anything else in your size, I'll be sure to let you know."

Francie took the clothes home and hung them in the closet, putting the shoes on the floor next to her bedroom slippers. Down in the bottom of the sack she found a little blue purse that Martha must have tucked in.

It felt good just to know there was something pretty in the closet. Every now and then, she took a break from studying to pull the closet curtain back, just to admire them hanging there.

"Well, did he ask you out?"

Julie cornered Francie the next morning when she came to work, before she could even close the door behind her. She asked the question within earshot of several customers

who were still drinking coffee and eating do-
nuts but glanced up, interested in knowing the
answer, too.

"Julie, not now," she whispered. "Let me
get my uniform on."

Julie followed Francie back to the tiny al-
cove in the back and stood outside the curtain. "Well, did he?" she demanded.

"Yes, he did." Francie mumbled as she
pulled the uniform over her head.

"Whoopee!" Julie shouted.

"Hush, Julie," Manny said. "The customers are wondering what's going on."

"Let them wonder," Julie replied, shushing
him. "This is important." As Francie emerged
from the dressing room, Julie said, "Tell me
everything. When? Where are you going?
How did it happen?"

"Friday for dinner. I'll tell you more when
we get a break. I promise, but I see the lunch
crowd coming in."

"Forget the lunch crowd." Julie waved her
hand at the customers crowding in the door.
"I want the facts."

Both Manny and Francie stared at Julie.

"What do you mean, 'Forget the lunch
crowd'?" Manny asked. "You've never said
anything like that in your life."

"I know." She put her hands on Francie's shoulders. "You are such a great kid, and I want you to be happy. I'm hoping this Fairchild is the one for you. He's a Christian, which is important to you, and he's a real hunk."

"Thanks, Julie." Francie hugged her boss. "Now," she said as she tied her apron behind her, "I have to get busy or I won't get any tips, and I really need tips."

She should have known her boss hadn't finished pumping her for information. As they wiped down tables, Julie said, "What're you going to wear? Your blue shirt?"

"I got a new outfit. A silky blue shirt and a dark blue skirt. Even new shoes."

"Where'd you get the money for that?" Julie studied Francie as if she was trying to figure out where any extra money would come from with Francie's tight budget.

"It didn't cost much."

"All that didn't cost much?" Julie squeezed her sponge out but kept her gaze on Francie.

"No. I got them at the church thrift shop. The ladies were so nice. One of them sewed a new collar on the blouse because the original collar had a stain on it, and they gave me a fifty percent discount."

"Those were ladies from your church? How nice of them."

"Yes, they are. This church has the nicest people, Julie. I wish you'd come."

But Julie didn't agree or refuse, she just changed the subject. "I bet you'll look great."

Friday afternoon, when she got home from work, Francie took a quick shower and washed her hair before settling down to study a little more and let her hair dry. At six-thirty, she ate a piece of toast. No use allowing her stomach to growl because she was eating so late, two hours past her normal time.

Makeup didn't take long. A puff of powder and apricot lipstick. Once she'd put on her blouse, Francie draped a towel over her shoulders and brushed her hair, curling it around her face—not that the effort tamed it in the least, but most of it was going in the same direction.

It took only a minute to pull on her skirt and slip into her new shoes. The shoes fit pretty well. Although they were a little large, they had elastic in the back and across the foot which kept them from slipping. The blouse fit nicely, the collar was pretty and feminine, and the skirt flared around her gracefully. Well, she thought it did but wasn't sure. She had to jump to be able to see the skirt in the small bathroom mirror.

She was ready fifteen minutes early.

With a pat to her springy curls, she turned back to the living room and picked up her history book to read while she waited.

After reading the same page twice, she tossed it on the chair. For some reason, the birth of a nation, important as it was, couldn't hold her attention. She stood and went to the window. There was no view of the front of the building from there. Actually, there was no view of anything except trash cans from here, so she had no idea why she bothered to look out.

Thank goodness there was a knock at the door at only a minute past seven.

Brandon had tried to pick out something not too dressy but not too casual to wear. Something that would show he was pleased to be going out with Francie, but that wouldn't make him look overdressed. Finally, he pulled out a pair of khakis and a blue knit shirt.

Should he drive? His car wasn't all that flashy, but it had cost more than the average parole officer could afford. He'd bought it with some of a trust his grandfather had set up for him.

Did Francie know he was pretty well-off? She had been a con artist. Maybe she'd checked his background, picked him out and done her pitiful but admirable act for him, to con him out of money or to marry a man who could give her a better life?

That was idiotic. Why would anyone check the background of a parole officer? No one at the office knew he had a little money. No one would care—and no one would tell one of their parolees, either.

And no, he didn't think Francie was conning him. He didn't have enough money to tempt a con artist. More importantly, she'd worked too hard at her transformation to be running a con game. What would she gain from it?

Should he wear a tie? Then he glanced at himself in the mirror and realized he was wearing a knit shirt. Why was he so nervous? He shook his head before checking his watch. He might as well go now. Drive slowly, get there a little early, maybe.

He pulled into a parking place about a block from the apartment, out on a busy street and under a street light. Swinging out of the car and locking it at a few minutes before seven, he strolled toward her building.

Although he should have to buzz her apartment to be allowed to enter, the front door was propped open with a brick. Really safe. He'd check her locks again to see how strong they were.

As he climbed the dimly lit steps he worried, too. There could easily be someone in the shadows, a thief or a rapist.

He hated that she lived here, but what could he do about it? Only encourage her to get an education so she could move out someday.

For a minute, he stood in front of Francie's apartment before lifting his arm to knock. Oddly, he felt this was a very important moment, an event which could change his life. Shrugging the foolish thought off, he knocked.

Francie opened the door wearing a blouse and skirt he'd never seen before. She looked nice. He looked from her head to her toes, noticing she had new shoes.

"Wow, you look beautiful, Francie," he said.

"Thank you." She twirled before him so he could see her skirt flare out. "I feel pretty tonight."

"That's because you are. You always are."

He wished he'd brought something. She would have loved flowers. Instead, as he entered the apartment, he turned to inspect the door. It wasn't very strong. He could probably beat a hole in it with one good blow of a hammer or from his fist. Then he inspected the locks. Two wobbly deadbolts and a flimsy chain. He'd have to put in something better. "Don't you have a peephole? How do you know who's out there before you open the door?"

"Usually I don't open the door, unless I'm expecting company. I figure if someone's out there they must have the wrong apartment."

He nodded. "Are you ready?"

She gave him a smile that lit up her face and shared her delight with him. He didn't think he'd ever get tired of such a simple pleasure.

She picked up her purse and said, "Ready." After closing and locking the door behind her, she took the hand he held out to her.

"I don't like these dark steps, either." He steadied her, afraid she'd fall although she'd made it up and down these rickety stairs hundreds of times without him.

"This is the low-rent district, Brandon. I'm

lucky to have lights. I carry this with me, if I know I'm going to be out late." She showed him her keys with a small flashlight on it. "It isn't much, but I can see the corners with it."

He wasn't convinced.

"And I scream very loudly. It's a talent I picked up when I lived with Uncle Lou. He was nearly deaf."

"I still don't like it."

"Also, Mr. Hobbs lives by the front door. When I come in late, I knock on his door. He listens to make sure I make it upstairs."

"Is this Mr. Hobbs strong? Could he beat up anyone who bothers you?"

"Mr. Hobbs is seventy, but he can use a telephone very well."

When they reached the first floor, Brandon decided to stop asking questions. There wasn't a thing he could do except brace Francie's door, make sure she had good locks and hope Mr. Hobbs didn't sleep too soundly.

"My car's around the corner," he said, keeping her hand in his.

"Is that your car?" Francie said when she saw the lone vehicle on the street. "It's beautiful."

"Thanks. I've had it for five years. My sister says I should get a new one, but this car runs fine and it's very comfortable." He opened the door for her and handed her inside.

Once in the car, Brandon watched Francie look around the interior.

She rubbed her hand across the leather seats. "Brandon, this is such a lovely car." Leaning back, she used the lever on the side of the seat to adjust it, up and down, forward and back.

"It's been a long time since I've been in a car that wasn't stolen," she said.

"That's probably not the best thing to say to your parole officer."

"Former parole officer." She looked up at him. "Besides, I was joking."

"I know, but being a parole officer is a hard habit to break." He put the key in the ignition.

"It might be easier if we pretended you don't know I was an ex-con and I can forget you were my parole officer." She placed her hand on his arm. "If we did that, maybe we could get to know each other like normal people get to know each other."

"Oh, you're saying we're not normal?" He started the car and checked the road behind him before pulling out of the spot.

"That's exactly what I'm saying."

"Okay, let's give it a try."

In only a few minutes, he turned into the parking lot of a popular family restaurant. "How's this?"

"Looks nice," she said in a soft voice.

He turned the engine off and got out of the car to open Francie's door, but she slid across the seat and out the door behind him.

He took her hand and they walked into the restaurant, together.

Chapter Nine

Once seated, Francie looked around, delighted to have someone else waiting on her, handing her a menu, filling her glass. Then she glanced at her menu. Her father had always ordered ground beefsteak because he'd said no one could ruin a hamburger steak. She bet he'd changed his mind after a few months in prison.

How much should she order? She glanced at Brandon. His car wasn't that new, but his shirt looked nice. And he wore that expensive-looking watch. She looked down at the menu again. "I think I'll get the spaghetti. Do you think it comes with a salad?"

"Francie, order anything you want. I can afford spaghetti *and* a salad. Do you want an appetizer? They have great Texas toothpicks."

She loved the deep-fried breaded onions and jalapeño strips but hadn't eaten them in years. "Are you sure? I don't want to be greedy."

"I'm positive. You're the least greedy person I know, but, I warn you, I love this appetizer. You're going to have to fight for your half."

Once the waitress had taken their orders and brought their tea and water, Francie leaned back against her chair. "You can't imagine how much fun this is."

But conversation flagged after that. Maybe she'd made a mistake, putting their relationship as parolee and parole officer off-limits, but if they had nothing else to talk about than her criminal record, it was probably a very good idea to discover that now. Of course, she could sit and stare at Brandon all night, but she didn't figure he'd enjoy it nearly as much as she did.

What did normal people talk about?

"Tell me about your family," she said as the waitress placed the appetizer in the middle of the table. "Do you have brothers and sisters?"

"Two sisters, both younger than I am. Miriam is married to her high-school sweetheart who's also my best friend. She and Phil have two children and another on the way."

"Do you like children? Are you a good uncle?"

"When I have time, but they're too young to do much with, like fishing or playing baseball."

"When is the next one due?" She nibbled on a slice of jalapeño.

"Some time in November."

"And your other sister?"

"Susanne is sort of the wild child of the family. Not in a bad way. She's a very independent woman who knows her own mind. It's hard to know what she'll do next, but she has lots of fun and make us laugh.'

"Is she married?"

"No, and the way she breaks hearts, I doubt if she ever will be."

Not that she'd ever meet them, Francie knew, but it was so much fun to hear about a real family, people who were together enough and who enjoyed each other so much that they smiled when they thought about each other, the way Brandon was smiling now.

"What are your parents like?"

"They're terrific people and true Christians. They raised us to care about other people, to help others."

"You're very fortunate."

"I know. Their example is probably the reason I'm a parole officer."

Their entrees came then, Francie's spaghetti and Brandon's grilled salmon.

For a few minutes they ate in silence, until Brandon said, "Now, I want you to know I'm not asking you this as your parole officer but as your friend."

She held her breath. Had he heard about Tim? He couldn't possibly know she'd had the gun, could he? Or was there a problem with something she didn't know about?

"What have you heard about your vocational counseling?"

What a relief! She allowed herself to breathe again. She didn't like keeping a secret, but she had to protect Tim. "I had an appointment last week. I took a bunch of tests, personality profiles and several—oh, what did they call them?—appraisals of vocational interest."

"How did they turn out?"

"I don't know yet. They were boring to take, but worth the time if they can give me direction. I have an appointment Wednesday to get the results."

She put her fork down and reached her hand across the table, placing it close to his plate. "Thank you again for setting all of this up. I've been so confused about where I should go, what I should do, if I can get a job I'd enjoy. You know, I'm going to have to make some choices about classes when I finish my basics, and that's not too far away."

"I'm glad I could do it." He put his hand over hers and squeezed it before returning to his meal.

After dinner, they strolled around the residential streets in the area, chatting and sharing interests, surprised to find they both liked art, although with Francie's background, that wasn't odd. "After all," she said, "I lived with an artist for years."

"Let's go to the museum next weekend," Brandon said. "I hear the Blanton over on the University of Texas campus has a great traveling exhibit of medieval European art coming in. Would you like to go?"

"I'd love it," Francie answered, delighted not only that she would get to see the art, but that he wanted to go out with her again.

"Have you been to that museum before?"

"Oh, several times, with my aunt. It has wonderful exhibits."

At ten, they walked back to the car and drove to her apartment. Brandon walked her up the three flights and watched as she unlocked the door.

"I'm going to get plywood to strengthen that door and a couple of better locks," he said. "Would it be okay it I came over some day to work on it? I'll let you know before I come."

She nodded while she put her keys in the little purse, closed it, and looked up at him. Surprised to find him so close, she started to take a step back but there was no room. Before she could move, he took her shoulders in his strong but gentle hands, leaned down and kissed her, softly and sweetly. His lips were like velvet against hers, and yet they were warm and loving.

Had she ever been happier in her entire life?

"Good night, Francie."

He leaned back and moved his hands from her but continued to gaze at her with an affectionate glow in his eyes. At least, Francie thought that was what she saw but it was hard to tell in the dark hall.

"Good night." She paused with her hand on the doorknob, not wanting to break the fragile connection between them.

"Make sure you turn all the locks." He turned away.

She watched as he went down the steps,

not entering the apartment until he disappeared from view in the murky depths of the stairwell.

The glow from the kiss lasted throughout the weekend. On Saturday, Francie had to force her brain back to math and history.

Of course, Sunday morning was church. As Francie meditated before the service, she looked up to see Julie settling in next to her. Francie grabbed her boss's hand and squeezed it.

"Don't get too excited," Julie whispered. "I thought I'd try it. Just *try* it, remember. Besides, I'm really here to find out how the date went."

Francie had never seen Julie in anything but a uniform. Today she wore a beautiful red suit and matching high-heeled pumps.

After the service, Francie introduced Julie to the minister, then stood in the open area outside the front door and chatted with some of the friendly people there.

"Well, I have to admit, they're nice people," Julie said as they moved toward the street. "Now, tell me about your date."

"Oh, Julie, it was wonderful!"

"Go on."

"We went out to dinner and talked." She smiled. "We got along well."

"Go on," Julie prompted.

"I'd love to tell you more. Tomorrow, I promise, but I have so much studying to do today."

"Okay, Francie." Julie studied her. "If you need to study, I'll let you go." She leaned toward Francie. "But I'm not going to forget. You can try to put me off, but tomorrow I'm getting the whole story."

"Now tell me everything. How'd your date go?"

It was Monday morning and, again Julie put down two cups of coffee and a slice of pie. Then, as usual, she slid into the booth across from Francie and shoved the plate and fork toward her.

True to her promise, Julie hadn't forgotten that she expected all the details and wouldn't be satisfied until she heard them all.

"I don't need pie," Francie mumbled.

"You're too skinny. It's my duty to fatten you up, and we've got plenty of leftover pie."

Francie looked up from the notebook where she was attempting to solve an alge-bra problem. "Our date was lovely. Absolutely wonderful." She grinned before looking back down at the stubborn equation.

"You can't stop there. Tell me more. What did you do?" Julie stirred sugar into her coffee and kept her eyes on Francie.

"Not much. Went out for dinner at that restaurant over by the mall, then walked around for a while."

"You looked great at church. Was that what you wore on your date?"

"I thought I looked nice." She smiled. "I thought I looked the best I ever have."

"And you had a great time."

"How could you tell?"

"You're glowing. Your eyes are sparkling. I can tell how happy you are." Julie shook her head. "I don't know how you ever managed to con anyone. Everything you feel shows up on your face."

"That was the secret. Always be the same, show all your emotion and people will believe anything you tell them, even if it's a terrible con." She shook her head. "That's a talent I'll never use again and don't want to pass on to anyone. Forget what I told you."

"Like I'd ever try to rip anyone off." Julie watched Francie for a few seconds before she scooted out of the booth. "You look nervous, kid, like you really need to get back to your studying."

With a sigh, Francie said, "I'm finding this algebra really hard. I never had much math because I didn't stay in school or study long enough for that. The history and Spanish aren't too bad, but this math might just do me in."

"Why don't you ask Tim or Mike to help you? I bet they still remember it."

"Thanks. I'm going in for a tutorial class tomorrow night. I'll see how that goes."

"Glad you had fun with your boyfriend, Francie. You deserve a little."

What had Julie said? Her boyfriend? The idea that Brandon was her boyfriend—well, she'd never considered it. Was he her boyfriend? She didn't know. She'd never had one, but she didn't think a man like Brandon would ever consider an ex-con his girlfriend.

But, if not, why was he spending time with her? Taking her to the museum and planning to fix her door?

Why had he kissed her?

Well, it was only a kiss. She'd heard a kiss didn't mean as much to a man, but what she thought she'd seen in his eyes contradicted that. She thought he'd liked it. No, she knew he'd liked it.

Of course, she didn't have much experience with that. She could count the number of men she'd kissed on her fingers. Deciding that Barry Greenwell in first grade didn't really count dropped the total to five.

And none of those other kisses were nearly as nice as this one, as Brandon's.

Feeling a little better about algebra after her class and the study session the previous evening, Francie could hardly wait for her appointment with the vocational counselor.

The office was in a building a block over from the building housing the parole office. The reception area was nicer than that of the parole office. In fact, the entire place was nicer, probably because it was a private agency. There were fairly comfortable chairs, the floor was covered with a dark rug, and magazines were stacked on a low table. Francie passed a few minutes glancing through a news magazine before the receptionist called her to meet with Miss Skinner.

Gray-haired, round and friendly, Miss Skinner stood and welcomed Francie with a smile. Once settled, she opened a folder.

"I see yours is a special situation. There arc some positions that, with your criminal record, you are excluded from. Fortunately, I don't believe you would find those interesting. Your interest in science and math is low, so medical and business professions would probably not appeal to you. However—" she turned a page "—there are some aptitudes you might wish to pursue."

Francie scooted her chair closer to the desk.

"Art," said Miss Skinner. "You have a high interest and aptitude for art." She looked up. "Have you ever considered a job in that field?"

Francie sat back, amazed. Perhaps art ability was as hereditary in her family as that propensity to break the law. "My aunt was an artist. She was really good, but she couldn't make much money selling her paintings."

"No, selling your own work is not a lucrative field for most artists. However, there are occupations which use art: design in many fields, window dressing, illustrating. We could look into the possibilities for these, if this field interests you."

"It does. I've always loved art."

"We could also look into computer-generated art."

"I'd like that. I had some computer courses when I was in prison."

"Have you taken any art classes?"

"No. My high-school career wasn't very successful. I cut classes and flunked English and math so often, I was constantly playing catch up. I never had time for the fun classes."

"Perhaps you would like to try one next semester. Computer art might be a perfect combination for you, maybe even animation." She turned another page. "Also, you show a high interest in writing and persuasion."

"Oh, yes, I can be very persuasive. It would be nice to use that for a legitimate career."

"Perhaps you could consider a career that used those interests, such as writing copy or advertising."

"It all sounds so interesting."

"I did find some areas of significance in your personality profile. You are energetic, optimistic, outgoing, but lacking in trust."

Francie didn't dispute that.

"Looking at the information Mr. Fairchild sent over, I can understand why." Miss Skinner leaned forward and met Francie's eyes. "I truly believe you will be able to find and hold gainful employment. We just have to find an area that interests you and get you trained for that. You sound responsible and motivated."

She closed the folder and clasped her hands on top of it. "What do you think?"

"I'm really happy about what you said and your suggestions. I love art. I'd like to look into professions in that field."

"Then let's make another appointment for you in…" She paused and scanned the calendar on her monitor. "I can't believe this month is so full. Guess it will have to be the twenty-third of next month."

She wrote the date on a card and handed it to Francie.

"Before you come back, I'd like you to go to the library or do an online search for professions that use art. Find out what the requirements are and if you feel you could handle them. I'll come up with some ideas, too."

"That's sounds great."

They shook hands. "It's been a pleasure talking to you, Miss Calhoun. I wish you the best."

Francie nodded in reply. "Thank you, Miss Skinner. I will certainly be trying to do my best."

When Brandon picked her up on Saturday morning, Francie was waiting for him on the street, glowing and almost dancing. She wore jeans, her new shoes and the blue shirt with the white collar he remembered. Yes, he knew pretty much every article of clothing in her small wardrobe.

"Why are you so happy this morning?" he asked as she got in the passenger side of the car without waiting for him to come around and open it for her, without even waiting for him to turn off the engine.

"Oh, so many reasons. You and I are going to the museum. I had a wonderful appointment with my vocational counselor who says I might actually be able to get a job in the future—a job I like." She turned toward him and laughed. "And I got 85% on a quiz in algebra."

He had to smile with her. In the short time he'd known her, he discovered he liked to look into her thoughtful eyes, to listen to her voice as she struggled with new ideas, and to laugh with her when she was so completely delighted with life. He liked it a lot. More than he should? More than either of them were ready for?

"That calls for a celebration. I'll take you to lunch in the museum café. If they don't have one, we'll find a special place." He started the car.

"Oh, you don't have to do that."

"I know I don't, but I want to. I like doing

things with you. I like to share your happiness." He pulled the car out into the street. "What did the vocational counselor say?"

"Miss Skinner said I don't have much interest in math and science, which was not exactly a surprise." She gave him a rueful smile. "She found out I do have a high interest and ability in art and writing. She thinks I could go into a number of fields with art." The air sparkled with her excitement. "I'm going to do some research on my own, and she's going to give me some suggestions and guidance."

"Francie, that's wonderful. What a great coincidence we're going to the museum."

As they wandered through the museum, she considered that people probably thought she had a boyfriend. With a glance at Brandon, she wondered if she did. He was holding her hand, seemed happy to be there with her, but did he care about her in that way? The way a man felt about a woman?

He'd said he was attracted to her. As good as that sounded, maybe that wasn't the entire reason he asked her out. Could it be she was one of the projects his parents had told him a Christian took on? Oh, she thought with a shudder, she hoped that wasn't the reason they were wandering around the gallery hand in hand.

They followed the arrows to the traveling exhibit area where Francie stopped and gasped at the beauty of the pieces: illuminated manuscripts in airtight glass boxes, tapestries, altarpieces, furniture, gold and silver work, carved wood, mosaics and murals. Tilting her head, she attempted to take in the enormity of the magnificence.

The art of Lorenzetti, Giotto, Holbein, Raphael and a tiny detail of a Jan van Eyck surrounded them. Oh, not major works by these artists. Those were all in important museums, but these were lovely examples nevertheless.

"Aren't they glorious?" She pointed toward one of the paintings. "See that wonderful blue? It's called 'blue from beyond the sea.' It's made from lapis lazuli and was incredibly expensive, but it was a far better color than had been used before.

"And look at the detail on this tapestry." She leaned forward. "The colors are so deep and vibrant, even after all these centuries." She turned toward him. "Isn't it marvelous?"

Brandon shook his head. "You don't just like art. You're an expert."

"No, not really." She smiled ruefully. "I know all this because I loved Aunt Tessie. Her sons didn't like art so she took me to museums a lot." She glanced up at him. "You don't want to know why she went to museums all the time, but I'm glad she took me along. She knew so much and taught me as we walked, pointing out technique and color and use of light. I learned so much, the difference between impressionism and post-impressionism, art nouveau and art deco. Probably my love of art came from her."

They wandered through the galleys, Francie pointing out the artists' use of light and other techniques. She surprised herself by how much she remembered.

As they started to leave, Francie stopped and grabbed his arm. "Brandon, do you think they have art classes here?"

"I don't know. I know they offer classes at the Austin Museum downtown."

"They do?" After a pause, she shook her head. "They're probably too expensive for me, but wouldn't it be wonderful to take a beginning art class? I'd love that." Maybe she'd check. It could be that she could take one or two, just to see if they fit her.

"You know, there are probably funds you

could apply for, maybe through the state rehabilitations commission for training."

Brandon always had the best ideas. She'd look into that with Mrs. Rivera and Mrs. Skinner.

For lunch, Brandon took her to a tiny café close to the campus. While she finished her quiche, Brandon said, "Tell me more about your aunt. She certainly taught you a lot. If she was so knowledgeable, how did she slip up?"

"She had a request for a piece that wasn't in the period she did best, that she knew most about."

"What was that?" He looked over at Francie.

"You've seen the paintings in my apartment. Her impressionistic work was glorious, but someone wanted a Dutch master, dark and gloomy. Unfortunately, the light from the impressionist style glowed in that painting. Obviously a forgery." Biting her lip she said, "It may have been she was tired of that life, that she hoped to get caught so she didn't have to keep painting forgeries. Whatever the reason, she's paying for it, and so are her sons."

He put his hand over hers. "I'm sorry I brought up the subject. I didn't mean to upset you."

"You didn't, not really. Most of the memories of Aunt Tessie are good."

Sunday morning was Francie's second time in the new Bible class. It was taught by an associate minister, Thomas Campbell, a young man who seemed to know a lot about the Church and Christianity, but who also encouraged everyone to participate. She felt safe, knew he wouldn't laugh at her if she asked a stupid question.

Not that she'd asked anything yet. She didn't know enough to think of a question other than, "What's Christianity all about?" but she listened and discovered that her Bible reading was beginning to connect with the discussion.

However, most of the material had to do with the section called the New Testament. She'd been trudging through Leviticus, which she was finding difficult. On top of that, and as much as she hated even to think this about the Bible, Leviticus wasn't nearly as uplifting as she'd hoped.

She decided to leap ahead in her daily reading to Matthew and go back to Leviticus when she had a better understanding and background. Meanwhile, she listened to the discussion, the questions the class asked and Reverend Campbell's answers.

During the service, the congregation sang the hymn she'd first heard at the revival service, "Amazing Grace." Today she shared a hymnal with Julie and sang out with pleasure as she remembered the change in her life those words had brought about.

After the service, as she and Julie moved toward what she'd learned to call the narthex but had always thought of as the lobby, she was startled to see Mike waiting for her.

"Hi, Francie. You're looking great. I like that outfit."

"What are you doing here?" Francie put a hand on his arm.

He shook his head. "I honestly don't know, but you talked about church, about the difference it was making in your life, so I decided to come. I wanted to sit with you, but I got here late and ended up in the back."

"Are you glad you came?"

"I don't know." He shrugged. "It's new. I liked it, but I don't know if this is going to mean as much to me as it does to you."

"Will you give it a chance? Come next week and sit with me? Change doesn't come right away. It takes time."

"I'll give it a try, Francie, but I've never been to church before—never had a reason to. This is important to you, and you know I'll do anything for you."

When the line reached the minister, Francie said, "Reverend Miller, this is my cousin Mike Fuller. He's studying to be a doctor."

"Good morning, Mike." Reverend Miller shook his hand. "We're glad you worshiped with us and hope you come back. We've enjoyed getting to know Francie."

"Yeah, she's a terrific lady," Mike said.

"And this is my boss, Julie…"

"Don't I remember you from last week?" the minister asked as he shook Julie's hand. "Glad to see you again."

"Nice place you've got here," Julie said, waving her hand toward the sanctuary. "Francie tells me you're a great bunch of people, and I'm beginning to believe her."

"We're very happy to have Francie attending regularly." He turned to take Francie's hand. "I'd like to talk to you about church membership. Maybe next Sunday?"

"Church membership? You mean there's more than just coming to church?" Francie asked.

"There's a lot more, but I don't want to

push you into anything. Why don't you stay for a half hour after church next week to talk about it with me?"

She nodded. Seemed like every time she thought she had this church thing figured out, there was more.

Once outside the church building, Francie turned to Mike and Julie. "I've got peanut butter and jelly at home. Why don't you let me fix you soup and a sandwich?"

"Love to," Julie said, "but I've got to clean my apartment this afternoon. If Mike can take you home, I'm going to take off."

When Mike nodded, she headed toward the parking lot, saying, "See you tomorrow."

They followed Julie toward the parking lot where Francie got into Mike's old clunker. It was fifteen years old and the fenders didn't match the body of the car, but it ran well because Mike was constantly tinkering with it. He said he hoped surgery would be as interesting.

When they arrived at Francie's apartment building, Brandon's car was parked there. Leaning against the car was, of course, Brandon. He wore soft, faded jeans and a burnt orange University of Texas T-shirt. Francie realized she'd never thought of Brandon wearing jeans, but he looked terrific and comfortable. Not surprising.

She felt a jolt of happiness to see him waiting for her.

"Wonder who that is and why he's here," Mike said. "The car and the guy look a little too high-class to be in this neighborhood."

When he saw Francie wave to the guy and the guy's answering smile, he asked with surprise, "Francie, do you know him?"

"Yes," Francie said and laughed when Mike's mouth fell open. Should she be insulted he was so amazed?

When Mike stopped the car, she got out to stroll over to Brandon. "What a nice surprise," she said.

Brandon eyed Mike. "Am I interrupting something?"

"This is my cousin Mike, Mike Fuller. I've told you about him."

Brandon relaxed and held out his hand. "Nice to meet you."

But Mike wasn't so quickly appeased. With a frown, he demanded, "Who are you?"

"This is Brandon Fairchild."

Dropping the hand Mike had never taken, Brandon said, "I used to be your cousin's parole officer."

"What are you doing here now?" Mike stepped between the two. "I wouldn't think Sunday would be a normal day for a parole officer to visit a parolee."

"Mike, he *used* to be my parole officer. He isn't anymore."

"Then why is he here?" He crossed his arms and glared at Brandon. "Are you hassling my cousin?"

Francie exchanged an amused glance with Brandon. "He's here because we're going out." When Mike still frowned, she added, "Together."

Mike swiveled to look at Francie. "You're dating this guy?"

She nodded.

"Francie, you never date," Mike said.

"Thank you for making me sound like such a prize, Mike," Francie said, but her smile softened the words.

"You are a prize, and I've never understood why you didn't date. You're a terrific person, but you always say you're too busy to go out."

"I'm glad she made an exception for me," Brandon said.

Turning back to Brandon, Mike said, "Francie's my favorite cousin. If you try any funny business—" He stopped to search for words. "You'd better not do anything to hurt her."

"I'm not into funny business."

"Mike," Francie interrupted, "I'm an adult. I can take care of myself. I appreciate it, but watching out for your womenfolk went out of style a century ago."

"Not with me," Mike said. He gave Brandon a meaningful glare and put his arm around Francie's shoulder.

"Mike, please stop." She groaned.

Then she noticed Brandon was trying to catch her eye and attempting not to laugh. "I came by to work on your door. Maybe Mike could help me," he said.

Mike faced Brandon. "Great idea. I've been meaning to do that." He studied Brandon again. "Could be you're a good guy."

"Could be." Brandon opened the trunk and handed Mike a toolbox and a rectangular piece of plywood. "I'm going to reinforce the door with that, then put on some better locks."

Mike nodded.

Then Brandon took out a larger bag, one with a great scent coming from it. "And I brought lunch. Hope you guys like barbecue."

* * *

After lunch, while Francie was washing the few dishes they had used and wiping the tablecloth, the two men started on the door.

"How'd you end up bringing Francie home today?" She heard Brandon ask. Not that she could help hearing the entire conversation in this tiny apartment.

"I went to her church," Mike mumbled through the nails he held in his mouth.

"I didn't realize you went to the same church." Brandon held the plywood against the door so Mike could nail it in place.

"We don't. I'd just heard Francie talk a lot about it, and church seemed really important to her now, so I decided to join her." He stopped working and took the nails out of his mouth. "Francie is the best person in the world. She's done everything so I can go to med school. I wouldn't have made it out of high school without her."

"Mike," Francie started to protest but Mike hurried on.

"So I figured if my going to church made her happy, I'd do it. Can't hurt."

"I bet she was glad to see you there."

"She was." Mike turned to look at Francie with so much love she had to smile back at him.

Then Mike put a nail against the board and

started to hammer. The two of them working together finished the job in less than thirty minutes. After that, they both had to show Francie how to lock the doors, as if she couldn't figure it out for herself.

When Mike left, Francie and Brandon drove around Austin, ending up at Zelker Park to amble hand-in-hand through the paths. By five, Francie had to go back to the apartment. Homework, she explained.

"Always homework," Brandon said.

After he walked her upstairs—despite her insistence that she could do this alone and he'd just have to go back down all those flights again—he stopped her protests with a kiss.

She watched him leave, thinking how foolish she'd been to want to walk the three flights of stairs to her apartment alone. She'd have missed the kiss.

She never wanted to miss one of them, not one. Who knew how many more there might be? Would there be more of those sweet, loving kisses? She needed to build up a surplus so when this ended—no one knew better than she that whatever was growing between the two of them had no future—she would have wonderful, sweet and loving memories.

Chapter Ten

"Okay," Julie said. "Remember your promise to tell me everything? How'd your weekend go? How was your day at the museum with the hunk?"

It was Monday morning. Again Julie put down two cups of coffee and a slice of pie.

"It was wonderful. The paintings were glorious." Francie answered evenly, even though the memory of the wonderful day made her want to grin. But, if she did grin, Julie would be hammering away for more details than she wanted to share. Instead Francie concentrated on her algebra.

"And the hunk?"

So much for her effort to distract Julie.

"He was nice, too." She pushed her book away and took a bite of rhubarb custard pie.

"Oh, he was nice, huh?"

"Yes, Julie, very nice."

"And the museum?"

"It was so amazing." Francie allowed her enthusiasm to show. "Did you know they have art classes there?"

Julie shook her head as she took a drink of coffee.

"I'm thinking about taking a beginning class," Francie continued. "To see if I have the ability and interest to do anything with art as a job."

"Isn't that terrific," Julie said. "Francie, I can't believe how your life is changing. When you first asked for a job, you were a little rough and skittish, like you didn't trust anyone."

"You tend to get that way in prison."

"Sure you do, but you were determined to change. I could tell. Even when you were really discouraged, you kept plugging away. I could see your potential, how you were working to turn your life around. Now you really have plans for the future." She patted Francie on the arm. "I'm excited for you."

"Julie, you're the one who gave me a chance. Thank you."

Julie shrugged and looked down at her coffee.

"Do you know what happened?" Francie went on. "I was working hard but really discouraged. What gave me the strength to keep going, to really turn my life around started with going to church."

"Francie, you don't have to try to convert me or convince me. I think you'd have made it without religion."

"Maybe, but my life seemed to fall in place after that. Faith gave me the courage to discover what I want to do and the strength to plan for the future."

"No." Julie shook her head. "I think you just fell in love."

Francie took another bite of the pie to give her time to consider that. After swallowing, she said, "I don't think so. Brandon would have made the appointment for the vocational counselor. He does that for lots of his parolees, but as far as him asking me out? I don't think he would have if I hadn't started going to church, if I wasn't really trying to change my life."

"Well, maybe so. Maybe not. Impossible to know now."

Julie started to slide out of the booth, but Francie kept talking. "I hope you'll come back to church Sunday."

"What are you trying to do, Francie?" Julie stood. "You know I like your church. Are you trying to convert everyone you know?"

"Why not? I've found something very precious. I want to share it with the people I love."

Sunday two weeks later, Julie missed church, but Mike slipped into the pew next to Francie. He'd come three times which warmed Francie's heart, but this morning he barely glanced at her and wore a grim expression, his lips tight.

"What's the matter?" Francie whispered as she handed him a hymnal.

"I'll tell you later," he said in a cold voice as he took the book but didn't join in the congregational singing.

When the service was over and after they'd greeted the ministers and their friends, Mike pulled Francie outside the church.

"What's the matter? Are you all right? Is Tim okay?" she asked.

"Tim told me what happened between you and him." He glared at her. "What in the world were you doing taking that gun? Francie, you're on parole. I know how much trouble you could get in."

"I couldn't let him keep it, Mike. You know that."

He shook his head. "You should have called me. I would have taken care of it. He's my brother."

"How could I get in touch with you?" She held her hands out in appeal. "It was ten o'clock in the morning. You were probably in class, and I was not about to let Tim go to school with a gun."

Mike walked down the sidewalk, looking as if he was trying to calm down. She followed him until he turned toward her.

"Francie, you shouldn't have to take care of us. You've got a life of your own."

"Mike, you and Tim are a big part of my life. There are times—in fact, almost always—when I believe you're the best part of it. I love you guys." She tried to put her hand on his arm, but he moved away.

"I love you, too, Francie, but I've got to start taking responsibility for my life and make Tim take responsibility for his. That gun stuff was just plain dumb."

"Mike, I'd expect you to understand better. At the time, there wasn't another choice. I thought then I was doing the right thing, and I still do."

"I know, Francie." This time he stopped pacing and took her hand. "You've always been great to us, but you've got school and work, and now this thing with your parole officer."

"But you're more important to me..."

"Francie, we shouldn't be. Your life is important, too. I want to help take some pressure off you so you can go to school, so you can find a good job." He put his hands on her shoulders. "I want you to be able to do what you want to do, maybe even have some fun."

She stepped back. "Are you telling me to stay out of your lives?"

"Of course not. I love you and appreciate all you've done for us. In the short time I've gone to church, I see why you like it. It's given me a center, but it's also made me realize how selfish I've been with my life, how irresponsible I've been."

"You're still a kid," she protested.

"Francie, when you were still a kid, you were taking care of me, getting me out of trouble. It's time for me to grow up and take responsibility for my life and for my brother." He held her gaze with his serious expression. "You have to allow me to do that."

"You're right." She shook her head. "I'm not sure I know how to sit back, but I'll try."

He put both arms around her. "I love you, Francie. I am grateful for everything you've done for me."

"I love you, too, Mike." Looking up at her cousin's face, she could feel tears fill her eyes. She dropped her head on his shoulder, and they hugged each other while Mike patted her on the back.

"Am I interrupting something?" Brandon's low voice came from behind Francie.

"Hi." She wiped her eyes as she turned. "What are you doing here?"

"We got out of church early today so I thought I'd come down and see if you needed a ride home."

Mike let go of Francie and she moved toward Brandon.

"What's the matter?" Brandon asked, taking out a handkerchief to wipe her eyes. He glanced at Mike. "Did something happen?"

"No," she said. "Well, not the way you mean. Mike was just telling me he's all grown up." Francie gave Brandon a watery smile. "It's hard when the young ones leave the nest."

Brandon handed her his handkerchief while he put his arm around her shoulder.

"So, where's this relationship between the

two of you going?" Mike asked, waving his hand at Francie and Brandon.

"Mike, I accept you as an adult, but that doesn't give you the right to meddle in my life. I've told you that before."

"I know, Francie, but I'm your oldest non-incarcerated relative. I only—"

"Your interest is appreciated," Brandon said in that cold voice Francie remembered from their second appointment. "But this is between Francie and me."

"Yes, sir. Sorry." Mike nodded but his lips curved a little at Brandon's tone. "Guess everything is under control." He leaned down and kissed Francie on the cheek. "If you've got a ride, I'll go on home." Walking away, he said, "See you."

She waved as he drove off, then turned to Brandon. "How nice to see you. I'm really glad you came by. What's the reason?"

"Church got out a little early today. No, that's not exactly right. I wanted to see you, so I sneaked out during the last hymn to try to catch you here."

"Oh?" She didn't like the serious note in his voice.

"There's a bench on the side of the

church—could we sit there for a little while?" He took her hand. "I'd like to talk to you."

Francie quickly glanced up, into Brandon's eyes. They, too, were serious, but his smile looked okay, not as if this was something terrible he wanted to discuss.

"That's fine."

In silence, they walked the few steps and sat down, side by side.

"Francie, your cousin asked a good question. It wasn't any of his business, but it's something I've been wondering. I think we need to talk about it, about us."

"I've had a wonderful time with you for the weeks we've been together. They've been magical." She said as she rubbed her thumb along the palm of his hand.

"Francie," he put his other hand on her cheek. "I care for you. I really do. You are sweet and smart and pretty. I'm so glad I've spent this time with you."

"But?" she prompted.

"But I don't know what's happening between us. I didn't think I'd learn to care about you so much and so quickly. We're so different." He stopped and looked in her eyes. "That worries me."

"You mean because I'm an ex-con?"

He hesitated before answering. "No, that's not it."

It was at least part of his confusion, her brain warned her.

No, not with Brandon. He wouldn't hold that against her, the heart insisted.

"Maybe I should never have asked you out in the first place." He paused and seemed to be pondering his words. "I'm not sure I understand what's going on between us."

"Is that bad?" She guessed it was or he wouldn't look so serious.

"Yes and no. No, because you delight and surprise me as no woman I've ever known has done. But yes, because I like to be more in control of my life and feelings. You said this before, and I still don't know if we have enough in common to build on."

Francie knew that. He was so much better than she was.

No, he was not better than her. She had to remind herself that she, too, was a beloved child of God.

No, he wasn't better, but he had that education and a good job, on top of the nice car and great clothes.

They were very different.

"Brandon, are you rich?" She couldn't believe she'd asked that. How rude and intrusive.

"Not exactly." He didn't meet her eyes, and he put her hand down.

"What does that mean? Why are you being so hard to pin down today?"

"I don't know, Francie." He reached out to take her hand again but stopped. "As I said, I'm puzzled by how strongly I feel about you."

"Is that bad?" she repeated, but he didn't answer. Instead her returned to an earlier question.

"My family has some money. They're not rich, and I'm not rolling in money."

What did that mean? Where was the line between having money but not rolling in it? All the money she could roll in would be a few fives and some change. She couldn't even imagine what he meant.

"Where did you go to college?" She'd assumed it was the University of Texas. After all, they were in Austin.

"Princeton."

"Princeton? And you ended up a parole officer?"

"Francie." He took her hands. "That's what I wanted to do. Going to Princeton is a family tradition, but I knew I wanted a job where I could work with people."

"Why not the ministry?"

"That's wasn't me, Francie. That's not where I was called to serve."

"You were called to be a parole officer?"

He nodded. "Strange, but I think I was." Looking directly into her eyes, he said, "The fact I have some money isn't important to me. It makes my life easier. I can afford more, but that's not one of the differences that separate us."

He had to be nuts if he didn't think having money wasn't an enormous difference between them. Because he came from money, he could never comprehend what *not* having money was like. That fact alone created a huge gulf between them, but she wasn't going to mention that, at least not now. He'd figure it out soon enough. She thought maybe that and the ex-con thing caused his concern, but maybe he hadn't figured that out for himself yet.

"What are your thoughts on what's happening between us?" she asked. "Have you made any decisions?"

"I don't know." He paused again. "Maybe we should just see what happens. Even as confused as I am, I'm too happy when I'm with you to want to stop."

His serious expression changed to a smile and he took her hand. "I don't know what's bothering me. Maybe it's because on Monday I have to leave for a conference in Galveston—"

"Oh, that's too bad, being forced to spend a week in Galveston," she interrupted with a smile.

He ignored her and continued, "I'm leaving early in the morning and won't have time to see you until next weekend. Maybe I feel this way because I'm really going to miss you by then. What are you doing Saturday?"

"I'm going to see my father. I haven't seen him since before I was incarcerated."

"Why are you going after all this time?"

"I should go. He is my father." She sighed. "He's one of the only relatives I have. Almost everyone else skipped out or is in prison. Of course he is, too." She shook her head as she looked up at Brandon. "Another difference between us. None of your family has been incarcerated. Coming from a family like that doesn't say much about me.

"Francie, you know it does. Look what

you're doing with your life in spite of all that. Be proud of yourself."

"Well," she confessed, "I am a little pleased, but that isn't a fruit of the spirit."

"Francie, you are absolutely overflowing with the fruit of the spirit." Brandon laughed as he pulled Francie to her feet. "Where is your father?"

"Hughes Unit, up in Gatesville," she said as they walked toward his car.

"Does your parole officer know you're going?" Brandon looked at her exactly like the parole officer he was.

"Yes, sir." She laughed up at him.

He joined her. "I'm sounding like your parole officer again, aren't I?"

"Mrs. Rivera and I discussed it. She believes it's important for us to keep the family tie, and she thinks I'm doing well enough in my rehabilitation to see him. She also reminded me I'm not supposed to have contact with felons other than my father, and that only in a supervised setting for short length of time."

He nodded. "Okay, sounds like you've got that taken care of. How will you get there?"

"Bus. It doesn't look like a bad trip," she added at his frown. "One change in Temple so I'm going to have to leave early. I'll take a book and study."

"How early will you leave?" he asked as they got into the car.

"About six."

"Why don't I take you?"

"Why would you want to do that? It'll be boring."

As he started the car, he turned to look at her. "First, I'd get to spend all day with you. That's always a good thing. Besides, if I drive, you can save a little money and get a little rest."

Then he smiled.

And, in that exact instant, Francie realized that, despite her fears, her doubts and all their differences, she'd fallen in love with Brandon. What she felt wasn't infatuation or admiration or being overwhelmed that a man like him showed her attention. It was love.

She knew she didn't love him because he was handsome—well, that wasn't the only reason—but because he cared enough to want to save her the time and hassle of a long day on a bus.

Being in love with Brandon—was that a good thing or a bad thing? Francie was not at all sure.

* * *

"Your car is much more comfortable than the bus." Francie leaned back in the seat. "Every time I've been on one, there have been screaming babies, people trying to sneak a smoke behind the seat, someone climbing over me to go to the bathroom or look out the window."

"I'm glad this is better than screaming babies and smoky air." Brandon looked over at Francie and enjoyed the sight of her. Wearing her blue blouse and navy skirt, she looked really pretty, but from her clasped hands he could tell she hid a lot of anxiety. "I thought the company might be better, too."

"Well, yes, the company is wonderful, but I think I might be happier about how quiet it is in your car."

He laughed. "If it gets too quiet, I've got music. I bet that's better than anything the bus offers. There're some CDs on your visor. Choose one."

"No, I'd rather talk to you. Do you mind?"

"Talking to you? No, I like that."

He drove for a few more miles and made a few comments about the traffic before noticing Francie wasn't keeping up her end of the conversation. Glancing over, he saw her head had fallen against the headrest. She breathed softly with her mouth open a little, sound asleep. She probably needed it, working her odd hours, taking three classes, watching over her cousins and trying to fit him into her schedule.

Was she cold? She wore only a light blouse, so he turned a little heat on and wished he had a blanket. There was one in the trunk, but he didn't want to wake her up to get it. So he drove in silence, looking over at her occasionally, enjoying the fact she slept so comfortably in the car next to him.

She woke up as he turned off the interstate and picked up Highway 36 to Gatesville.

"Sorry." Francie covered a yawn with her hand. "I wasn't very good company."

"You're always good company. Even when you're sleeping. I like to listen to you snore."

She glared at him as she sat up. "I do not snore."

"Well, not very loudly."

She rolled her eyes then turned to watch the scenery while the miles flashed by. As they approached Gatesville, Francie rubbed her hands together and answered Brandon's attempts at conversations with only a few words.

"Do you want to stop for coffee?" he asked.

"No," she said, then added, "Thank you. I don't want to be late."

He didn't tell her she had plenty of time. He figured as tense as she was, she didn't care.

She opened up the piece of paper with directions on it. "Follow thirty-six north of town and turn right on nine-twenty-nine. That's sort of northeast. She glanced over at him. "Of course, you probably know that."

"Francie, this is going to be okay." He took her hand.

"Of course it is. I'm sure of that," she agreed but her voice was shaky. "I'm just going to see my father."

He gently put her hand down and nodded.

After he turned off Highway 36, she said, "It should be about a mile and a half from this intersection." She clenched her hands in her lap, shredding the paper with the directions. When they saw the beginning of the high chain link fences surrounding the prison, she looked down and realized what she was doing, wadded the paper in a ball and put it in the litter bag before sitting absolutely still, hands folded again and eyes closed.

When he turned in the gate, she opened her eyes and took a deep breath.

Once through security and in front of the

main entrance, Francie asked, "What will you do while I'm inside?"

"I brought a book."

"Are you going to stay out here in the car?"

"Don't plan to. Secure facilities don't like a car running in the parking lot or even just a driver waiting." He opened his door and got out. "I'll find a place inside to read while I wait for you."

From the visitors' lounge, he watched Francie walk slowly toward the prison section, down a hall with scuffed vinyl tiles and tan walls toward a door with a guard next to it. Her shoulders were straight, her back rigid. With a glance over her shoulder, she went through the door, which closed behind her.

She was a strong person, he reminded himself. When he looked at her, he saw the curls and the big eyes and her gentle smile, but inside was a great deal of courage and toughness. And, now, faith.

"Merciful God," he prayed quietly, *"calm her and give her peace."* Then he bought a cup of thick lukewarm coffee from a vending machine and settled down with his book.

Sam Calhoun looked so much older than Francie'd remembered. When she'd been a child, he was a bear of a man with a full head of dark hair.

Even three years ago, he'd looked younger. Back then, he'd still had most of his hair with only touches of gray.

Now he was stooped and thin. His remaining hair was completely gray. Comparing him to the man who used to hold her over his head and swing her around when she was a child made the difference much more drastic.

"Hi, Dad," she said to the man who sat on the other side of the window from her.

"Hey, Angel."

She'd forgotten his nickname for her.

"How long has it been since I've seen you?" he asked.

"Three years? Maybe almost four?" She put her hand to the glass and he put his against it.

"Thanks for the letters, Angel."

"I should've written more." But it had been so hard to write someone she no longer really knew.

"I appreciated them. You kept me up with what's going on in the family. I feel isolated in here. Of course, that's one of the big problems with being in prison. I don't get out the way I used to." When he grinned, she could see her father in the smile.

"Mike's doing great," she said.

"Medical school is tough."

"But he's doing well. He's been going to church with me and is going to spend more time with Tim."

He nodded. "Glad to hear he's taken on that responsibility." After a pause, he added, "You're going to church now. Why?"

"I thought it was a good idea." How could she explain what had happened to her to a man who'd never been inside a church? "It makes me feel peaceful."

"Hey, going to prison can do that." He shook his head. "But if religion works for you, that's a better choice."

There was a long silence before Francie asked, "What do you do in here?"

"They've got some interesting programs. I work in the garden, took some courses in horticulture. A few years ago, I started literacy classes." He leaned forward. "Francie, did you know I didn't know how to read? They said I was functionally illiterate. Eight years of school, and I still couldn't read. That's why I dropped out back then. I tried to hide it, but if you can't read, it's hard to pass anything, hard to keep a job. Hard to hide it, even thought I tried."

"Really, Dad? I didn't know that. How are the classes?"

"You'd probably laugh at some of the things I'm reading, but I'm proud of being able to do it." His expression dared her to disagree.

"I'm proud of you, Dad. How's your health?"

"Pretty good for an old man. You know I'll be fifty-six on my next birthday? But my blood pressure is low and my health is good. I'm fine, and I plan to spend my fifty-eighth birthday with my family."

"I hope so, Dad."

They chatted a little longer, about his brother and sister and when they'd be out of prison, about not hearing from her mother for years and about her classes.

"You're taking college classes." He shook his head again. "I always thought you had the brains in the family. What do you want to do with that education?"

"I have an appointment with the vocational counselor soon. We're thinking about something in art."

"Just like Tessie, huh?"

"I hope not, Dad. I've spent enough time behind bars."

"Yeah, we all have." He said that at the same time the guard told him he had to return to his cell. Francie stood and waved before she turned toward the door.

Francie slowly walked down the hallway toward Brandon, her face almost as pale as the shabby floors. He hadn't been able to read much of his book because he'd kept looking up for her for the thirty minutes she was gone. When she saw him, she smiled, but it was a weak smile, a turning up at the lips with no real joy.

"How did it go?" He handed her one of her favorite chocolate candy bars. "I bought this for you from the vending machine."

"Thanks, but I think I'll eat it later." She slipped it in her purse before dropping into a chair. "It was fine. He looked good, but he's changed." She hesitated before adding, "Of course, after so many years here, I expected him to change. He was so big and strong, but now he's an old man who's spent most of his life in prison. What a waste."

He sat next to her and took her hand.

"Brandon," she said as she shifted in her chair and look up at him. "I could have ended up that way."

"No, Francie, you wouldn't have." He put his arm around her and she leaned against him.

She nodded, slowly. "Yes, I could have. I had no goals and no education or training of any kind. Even when I got out of prison and I knew I didn't want to go back, I didn't know how to go straight." She bit her lip. "I had absolutely no idea. What if I'd made the decisions he did? What if I'd gone back to crime?"

"Francie, you didn't. You had it rough, but you've worked hard. I've read your files. Even with the terrible notes Gentry kept, it was obvious you were determined not to go back." He lifted her hand to his lips and kissed it. "I'm going to help you stay straight if I have to spend every moment of my time with you."

"Thank you." She smiled. Her lips trembled, but at least the smile reached her eyes. "How nice to have my own personal parole officer. Thank you for sacrificing your time for that."

"It's no sacrifice. I can think of no place else I'd rather be." He put her hand against his cheek and held it there. "Let me take you home, Francie."

Chapter Eleven

At midnight a week later, the phone rang. Brandon struggled to wake up. A call in the middle of the night always scared him, especially since his father had had a heart attack three years earlier. He had to feel all over the bedside table looking for the phone. Grabbing the receiver, he mumbled a sleepy, "Hello?"

"Brandon Fairchild?" said a deep male voice. "This is Sgt. Fitzgerald at central booking. We have a young man here, a Sean McCray, who'd like you to come down here as soon as possible."

Brandon was immediately awake. "You're booking Sean?" He turned on the lamp and sat up. "What for?"

"Robbery. I can't tell you much more over the phone. Hold on," the sergeant said.

For a few seconds, all Brandon could hear was the sergeant talking to someone else in the background. Then he came back on the line, "Sorry, we're pretty busy down here. I'm only calling because the kid asked me. Said he'd like to see you."

"Thanks." Brandon hung up and got out of bed to throw on some clothing. After combing his hair, pushing his feet into dock shoes and picking up his keys, he ran out of his apartment.

When he arrived at the police station, an officer led him into a holding cell and left Brandon alone with Sean.

"I'll be right outside," the officer said. "Call when you're through."

Before Brandon could say a word, Sean said, "Mr. Fairchild, I didn't do this."

Brandon turned to look at Sean. The young man's blue eyes were wide and innocent. His freckles looked dark against ashen skin and his red hair was wild and uncombed.

"Mr. Fairchild, you know how honest I am, how hard I'm trying to change. Can you tell someone they've made a big mistake?"

"Why don't you tell me what happened."

Brandon leaned against a wall and watched Sean pace around the cell.

"I was asleep when there was a pounding on the door. I didn't answer it because I didn't know who it was."

"Who did you think it might be?"

Sean stopped walking and gazed at Brandon for a second before looking away. "I don't know. Maybe some old friends trying to get me in trouble. Could've been some bad dudes that live in the neighborhood."

"Go on."

"Before I could do anything, they knocked the door down. It was the police." He acted the scene out dramatically, imitating the knock at the door and his fear. "They cuffed me." He put his hands behind his back. "And brought me down here."

"Why do you think they did that?" Brandon didn't believe Sean, but he hoped his voice didn't show that. He'd seen a lot of cons who'd been arrested while on parole. Those few who were innocent had always been scared to death, afraid that they'd be put away again because they couldn't trust the system. Those who were guilty explained and explained.

"I don't know." Sean paused. "I think

someone snitched on me to take the heat off them. I must have been framed. I made a guy with a really bad temper angry last week. Could've been him."

Brandon listened but said nothing.

"Can I go home?" Sean asked.

"I'll talk to the sergeant."

Brandon turned and signaled the guard to let him out of the cell.

"Can you tell me what happened with Sean McCray? Why was he arrested?" Brandon asked the desk officer.

After scanning the report, the officer said, "We got a tip yesterday afternoon that the kid was involved in a series of robberies. Got a search warrant and went to his place last night. The officers heard someone inside. He didn't answer, so they broke in. He was trying to escape out the window."

Brandon nodded. "What did the officers find?"

"The bedroom was full of hot electronics. Computers, plasma-screen televisions, you name it."

"And you're sure Mr. McCray was involved?"

The sergeant approached the desk and said, "Not a bit of doubt. It was his apartment. It'd be hard to smuggle all that stuff into the only bedroom without the kid knowing. Bet his fingerprints are all over everything."

"What are his chances of getting out of here?"

"Not good. The only thing he has to bargain with is the names of his partners."

"Too big to be a one-man job?"

"Lots of heavy stuff in there," the sergeant answered.

"How long has this been going on?"

"We figure about five or six months."

From the time Sean had gotten out of prison. Was there anyone dumber and more stupidly trusting than he was? All those months, the kid had been telling him how much he was changing. And Brandon had believed him. Brandon always wanted to believe his clients. What an idiot he was. All Sean wanted from him was to get him out of jail. The kid was a user like most of his parolees.

Brandon took a sheet of paper from the desk and wrote two names: Jorge Barrios and Chester Robertson. As he handed it to the sergeant, he said, "First, you might want to call McCray's lawyer. Then you might want to talk to these men."

As he left the police station, Brandon muttered to himself, "When am I going to learn that an ex-con is a manipulator?"

Then Francie's lovely smiling face, her blue eyes and freckles, appeared in his thoughts.

On a Monday morning after Julie had come to church fairly regularly for almost two months, she slid into the booth with Francie, bringing the usual coffee and pie.

"You know, I like your church," Julie said with amazement in her voice.

"It's your church now, Julie."

"Well, maybe." She took a gulp of coffee and thought for a minute before she said, "I have a question. What was that fruit of the spirit stuff you talked about right after you went to church the first time?"

"In Galatians, Paul says that you know Christians by the way they act, by the fruit of the spirit."

"And what are they?"

"'Love, joy, peace, patience, kindness, generosity, faithfulness, gentleness and self-control.'"

"You know them pretty well."

"They're important to me. I read them so often, I memorized them."

"So, tell me this. Because you're a Christian, do you automatically get all that stuff? Even if you only go to church, do they become part of you? You know, like kindness and love and patience? Just *poof* and you've got 'em?"

"Julie, I don't know everything. I'm learning a lot about becoming a Christian, but I think you have to work to get them or, maybe, once you've found faith, they show up in the way a person acts."

"You're a new Christian, but you're way ahead of me." Julie bit her lip before continuing. "Does this all mean we're supposed to be kind and patient and all those other things to everyone, no matter how downright frustrating they are?"

"You mean Manny?" Francie whispered.

"Maybe."

"Well, whoever you're talking about, Julie, I believe that's exactly what it means."

Julie shook her head. "This church stuff of yours is hard. When I first went to church with you, I didn't think it meant I'd have to be polite to Manny or I don't know if I'd have started it." She looked over at the cook in the kitchen. "Don't know how he'd react if I started being patient and kind."

"The only way to know is to try."

"I don't think I'm far enough along the path to try that yet."

That evening, as she put the orders on the clips and picked up the hot plates from the counter, Julie watched Manny. How would he act if she started being nice to him?

"What's the matter," he asked as he handed her a number-three platter. "You keep looking at me."

"I was wondering if you got a haircut." That was dumb. According to health-department rules, Manny had to cover his hair. He wore a dark, almost invisible net, but she couldn't see enough to know if he'd gotten a haircut or not.

He shook his head and pulled down another order to fill.

"Anyway, you look nice." She grabbed a basket of biscuits and ran toward the booth.

Obviously she wasn't quite ready to start with the fruit of the spirit. Maybe little by little was the trick. She'd try again later, maybe with self-control, and work up to kindness and gentleness.

Two days later, she thought she was ready. After the last dinner customer had left and the dishwasher had mopped the floor and slipped out the back—and before Julie could lose the courage to approach him—she pulled a chair from a table. She waited there in the dark while Manny put his bean soup in the slow cooker to simmer overnight.

That finished, Manny washed his hands, grabbed his jacket, flipped out the light in the kitchen, and headed for the door.

"Just a minute, Manny," Julie said.

He turned around. "What are you doing here? I thought you'd left twenty minutes ago."

She stood to turn on a light. "I wanted to talk to you."

Manny took a step back. "What's the matter? Are you sick? Really sick?"

"No, I'm fine."

"Are you mad at me? Do I still have a job?"

"Of course you still have a job. You're the best cook in town. Why would I fire you?"

He shrugged. "I don't always understand you."

She started to fling an angry retort at him before she whispered to herself, "Peace, patience and self-control."

"What did you say?" He squinted in her direction as though he was trying to read her expression.

"Manny," she said, plowing ahead. "We used to be good friends. I don't know exactly what happened, but we aren't anymore. We don't even seem to like each other."

"You don't know what happened?" He threw his hands in the air as his voice rose. "You're hard to get along with, you're… "

"I'm guessing you think the reason we don't get along now is my fault. I really don't remember the argument that started this, Manny, but I'd like to be friends again. I'm sorry for anything I did, for anything that came between us."

"What?" He turned his head a little, still studying her. "Why are you saying this? What do you really want?"

"That's all I want. I want us to get along, not to fight all the time." She leaned toward him and spoke slowly and, well, patiently. "I'd like us to be friends again."

"We used to be more than friends. We were going to get married," Manny said softly. He watched her for a few seconds before he asked, "What about that?"

"I'm not asking for anything more than friendship. I miss you. I miss talking to you. More than anything, I hate fighting with you."

"You've been going to church with Francie, that's it. Isn't it? You're trying to be a good person, like Francie, right?"

She nodded. "I like church. I realize there are ways I need to change. And it makes me feel peaceful."

"Julie Sullivan peaceful? Not sure I believe that's possible."

She felt like throwing the chair at him, but she was sure that wouldn't show either patience or love.

She'd known it would be hard to apologize to Manny, but she hadn't realized how difficult it really was. She should have. Manny was as hardheaded as ever.

He thought for a moment. "Are you using me to get to heaven?"

"No, Manny." She struggled with her temper. "I'm reaching out."

He watched her, his dark eyes serious, but he didn't say a word.

"Well, you think it over, Manny. Remember I've taken the first step."

"Don't think you're going to get me to come to church, just because you're being nice."

"Manny, all I want is for us to get along. If you decide to come to church, I'd be really happy. You would be, too, but it's something you have to do for yourself." She pulled her key out and turned the light off. "Go on out. I'll lock the door behind us."

After he left, she looked down at the key ring, a flower imbedded in clear plastic. Manny had given it to her a year earlier, said she was his yellow rose.

Yes, she'd like to be more than friends, but if they could just speak to each other politely that would be a welcome change.

The lunch crowd was heavy today. Both Julie and Francie were running constantly. They'd even pulled Harold the dishwasher out to bus tables.

After Julie cleared a table, she started to lift the bin of dirty dishes while Harold cleared a booth for the waiting customers.

"Julie, don't try to lift that," Manny shouted. "You'll hurt yourself. Let one of the kids do it."

"I can…" Julie began angrily before glancing at Francie. Then Julie grinned. She guessed Manny was trying to be nice, even if he had implied she was too old and weak to handle the heavy bin. "Thank you, Manny," she said. "Harold, when you get finished with that, would you take these dishes into the kitchen?" She grabbed a rag, wiped the table, and dried it before seating the next group in line.

By one-thirty, the crowd had thinned. Hearing the door open, Francie looked up with a smile, hoping it was Brandon. Dropping by at this time had become a habit for him once or twice a week.

And it *was* Brandon. What a nice surprise.

"Hello, Julie and Manny," Brandon said as he seated himself at a table. "Francie, I'd like coffee and a piece of apple pie, please."

She brought him a mug then sat down across from him.

"Hey, Brandon," Manny shouted from the kitchen.

"Hello, Manny." Brandon nodded at both Manny and Julie before returning his attention to Francie.

"How're Tim and Mike? Do you hear anything from your father?"

"I haven't heard from anyone, so I'm guessing they're fine. How's your family?"

"My father's decided he wants to buy a sailboat. My mother's against it because she figures he'll never have time to use it. You know, normal family stuff." He took another drink of coffee.

No, she didn't know about normal family

stuff and the idea of a parent wanting to buy a boat of any kind or size amazed her, but she wasn't going to say anything about that. It would just be something else they didn't have in common.

"Speaking of family," Manny shouted from the kitchen, "you've met Francie's cousins, right?"

"I've met Mike, but not the other one." He glanced over to Francie. "What's his name?

"Tim," she said.

"Anyway, you've met a member of her family, right?"

Brandon nodded.

"So," Manny continued, "when are you going to take Francie home to meet your family?"

Julie swirled to glare at Manny while an embarrassed silence filled the diner. Brandon slowly cut himself a piece of pie with his fork, put it in his mouth, and chewed it, careful not to make eye contact with Francie.

"What are you saying, Manny?" Julie shouted. "It's none of your business." Then she closed her mouth and eyes. Francie bet she was reciting the fruit of the spirit to herself.

"Manny," Julie said in a sweet, gentle voice with only a hint of irritation, "that's none of our business. It's between Brandon and Francie."

"When I was young, it was considered the polite thing to do, to introduce your girl-friend to the family. How long have they been going out? Two months?" he asked Julie. "You ask me, it's time for him to do that, if he's a gentleman."

"No one asked you, Manny," Julie said.

No, no one had. Francie had always figured that when the time was right, she'd meet his family. If their relationship was going that direction.

But today that reasoning rang false to her. Why hadn't he taken her to meet his family? She realized the question had surfaced in her mind before, but she'd never really answered it, always rationalized that someday he would. Sounded a lot like what she'd learned in the psych class last summer. Denial.

"I've got to go." Brandon took a last drink of coffee and tossed some bills on the table. "I've got an appointment in a few minutes."

But Francie noticed he hadn't answered Manny's question.

After he left, she picked up the half-eaten piece of pie and shook her head. Then she looked up at Julie and Manny who were suddenly very busy pretending they hadn't noticed the same thing.

* * *

Swinging the racket with every bit of his fury and frustration in the stroke, Brandon hit the ball so hard it zipped back and almost took Phil's head off.

"Hey, buddy," his friend protested. "I don't know what's bugging you, but don't take it out on me." Phil tossed the ball back to Brandon. "Bang the ball around in here by yourself and call me when you're ready to play a friendly game that doesn't involve decapitation." He turned and stalked off the court

After hitting the ball against the wall for fifteen minutes, Brandon was covered with sweat and his shoulder was killing him, but emotionally he didn't feel any better.

He picked up the ball, left the court, pulled his towel out of his bag, then stuffed everything else inside. After wiping off his face and arms, he sat down on a bench outside the court, draped the towel over his shoulders and tried to come to grips with his feelings.

It all came down to the question of whether he could trust Francie, and there didn't seem to be a good answer. He thought he could, but logic told him most parolees lied and manipulated. Hadn't Sean? Hadn't hundreds before him?

But they weren't Francie.

His thoughts started tumbling in his brain, going round and round and coming out nowhere.

What was he going to do? He wanted to believe her.

Did he love her? He'd though maybe so, but how could he be in love with someone he couldn't trust?

"How's your math class going" Julie asked a few days later.

Francie shuddered. "It's taking a lot of work. Math really isn't my thing."

"Oh, you'll be fine. Look how well you're doing in all your classes."

"Yes, but this is really hard. I have to get busy." She turned back to her notebook.

Odd, but ever since Manny had asked Brandon about when he was going to take her to meet his family, Julie didn't ask questions about "the hunk" anymore. Well, not so odd. Julie and Manny had always been protective of her.

"Oh, by the way, I thought you might be interested to know that Manny and I are going to a movie tonight." Julie said as she picked up her coffee cup and headed back toward the kitchen.

Francie dropped her pencil and stared at Julie's back. "What?" she shouted, but Julie kept moving. Francie wasn't about to get up and demand to know what was going on with Manny when he was right there in the kitchen. Instead, she slid from the booth quickly and was attempting to pull Julie out of the kitchen when the phone rang.

"It's for you," Julie held the phone out. "It's what's-his-name."

And Julie never said Brandon's name anymore.

"Yes?" Francie said.

"Hi, Francie. Wanted to let you know that I won't be able to take you to dinner tonight."

His voice sounded a little rushed and troubled.

"What's the matter?"

"Nothing, I hope. My sister Miriam went into labor. Her husband rushed her to the hospital, and the family's meeting there. We're a little worried because she's early, but probably everything's fine. I'm going there right now. I'll let you know as soon as something happens."

"I'll keep her in my prayers."

"Thanks, Francie." He hung up

* * *

Francie finished work, went to class and walked home, hoping with every step that she'd look up to see Brandon waiting for her with good news about the new baby.

She didn't see him that day or the next, but when she'd finished serving breakfast and was studying, she looked up to see him standing next to the booth.

"Let me get you some coffee," she said, but Manny was there with a cup before Francie could stand. He glared at Brandon as he put the coffee on the table.

Brandon looked tired, but it was obvious he'd been home. His shirt was fresh and he'd shaved.

"How's your sister?" Francie asked.

"She's fine. Everyone's fine. I have a new little niece, Elizabeth Catherine, born yesterday afternoon at one-twelve." He stretched. "Sorry I didn't get here earlier. I was exhausted. Took two days off from work—yesterday and today—to rest up." He took Francie's hand. "She's a beautiful little girl. Weighs seven pounds and something. Healthy, and so is my sister."

"Was it a difficult delivery?" She sipped her coffee and watched him.

"Not bad, just long. Of course, I wasn't the one having the baby. This is her third child, so we knew the drill. The one who really went nuts was my sister's new boyfriend."

"Your sister's new boyfriend?" Francie put the coffee cup down and straightened.

"I don't know why Susanne brought him. They've only gone out three or four times. Jerry'd never been through a birth before. I thought he'd pass out when Phil came out with the details about what was happening."

"Your sister's new boyfriend was there?" she asked.

Brandon put down his coffee and glanced at her. At first he didn't grasp the reason for her question, but she could see that, little by little, he understood the implication.

"I thought you said only the family was gathering," she said.

"As I said, I don't know why Susanne brought him. It *was* just family, except for him."

"Except for Jerry." She looked Brandon in the eyes. "If Susanne brought her new boyfriend, why didn't you ask me to come?"

He didn't say anything, which seemed like a really bad sign.

"I would have come. You know that."

He nodded.

"You didn't want me there, did you?" When he still didn't answer, Francie said. "You don't want to introduce me to your family, do you? It's exactly as Manny said."

"It's not that I don't want to, Francie. It's that we're so—"

"So different?" She struggled to keep calm.

"Francie, you know I care about you." He reached over to take her hands, but she dropped them in her lap.

"Why don't we go see the baby now? I'd like to see her."

She never thought she'd see Brandon so uncomfortable. He refused to meet her eyes.

"Brandon, please look at me." When he did, she said, "You're afraid your family will be there, aren't you? Afraid that you'd have to introduce them to this ex-con who doesn't have nice clothes or much money, who has very little education and whose family is full of criminals?" She forced back the tears that threatened and sat up even straighter.

"Francie… " He struggled for words. "I care for you. You know that. I've showed you how much. I'm sorry I've hurt you, but I don't think this is the time to discuss this, I'm tired and you're upset. With everything that's going on, this isn't the time for my family to meet you."

"When would that be? When you can finally accept the fact that you're dating an ex-con you met when you were her parole officer?"

"Francie, I don't know how to explain." He leaned forward. "I've been confused about what's happening between us and didn't handle this well. I've struggled with my feelings and prejudice. I've prayed about it, but I'm not ready to tell my family about you."

"Are you ashamed to tell your family about me?"

He didn't answer.

Francie hadn't thought that anything could hurt more than when she had watched the cops drag her father out of the house, but this did. Anguish clamped down over her chest so hard she had to struggle to breathe. But she was *not* going to cry, not while Brandon was there.

"Then you don't have to." Francie bit her lip. "Being ashamed of another child of God—well, Brandon, I know I'm not supposed to judge, but I don't think that's what the Bible means by 'love one another.'"

"Give me some time, Francie."

"No, Brandon. You've had long enough."

She stood. "Now, if you'll excuse me, I need to start getting ready for the lunch crowd."

"Francie, they won't come in for another hour." He stood and followed her.

She turned to face him, struggling to remain calm and controlled. "I do appreciate everything you did for me. You encouraged me to read the Bible and to find a church. All of that changed my life. You took me to see my father. Thank you for all of that, but I will not allow you to look down on me."

"I don't… "

She didn't answer, just moved away and headed toward the kitchen with him following.

"Francie…" he tried again.

"Leave her alone," Manny stood in the door to the kitchen. "She said to leave her alone."

"I didn't hear her say that," Brandon said.

"Go away and leave me alone," Francie said. "Please," she added in a whisper.

He looked at Francie for almost a minute before he did what she'd asked.

When Julie arrived a little later, Manny hustled her into a corner of the kitchen and, Francie guessed, told her what had happened with Brandon.

After the lunch crowd thinned, and before

Julie could try to comfort her, Francie took off for class. She didn't think she could handle comfort now. She wanted to be alone, to think of something else, a new and better plan for her future, a future that didn't include Brandon.

But most of all, she wanted to pray for strength as she rushed to class.

Two weeks later, Maxine Kaplan stood in front of Brandon as his last appointment of the day left.

"What do you need, Max?" He pushed his notes aside and motioned her toward a chair.

"I'm worried about you." She sat down and pulled the chair closer to the desk. "You don't seem to be as—I don't know what word I want—*positive, enthusiastic,* maybe even *caring* with your clients for the past week or so."

Had it been that obvious? He'd felt as if he'd gone through the motions mechanically, not really caring about anything he'd done but still trying to do the best for his parolees. If Maxine had noticed, he obviously wasn't doing all that well.

"I'm a little tired," he said, pushing the folders to the side of his desk.

"I noticed the change right around the time

your sister had the baby. Is she all right? Is the baby okay? Are you worried about them?"

"No, Max, I'm just tired."

"Burned out?"

His glance leaped to her face. "I didn't think so. Why?"

"Brandon, you're the best parole officer we have. You know that, I know that, the other officers know that. Your parolees agree. You've been here longer than anyone else but me, but I've been doing administration for three years. You've been out here, doing the real work, the tough job."

"I'll remember that when I need a raise," he said in an attempt to make a joke. It didn't bring a smile.

"This is a high-stress situation. You get a lot of disappointment. Parole officers don't usually last here as long as you have. Those that do either don't do a very good job or they take very good care of themselves."

"I take good care of myself, Max. I eat right, I play racketball."

"Other people take vacations, Brandon. I checked. You have almost thirty days of vacation time built up. Last year you lost five days because you didn't take them." She leaned forward. "I know why you didn't take them.

You think your clients can't get along without you, but they really can't get along if you burn out. You've got to take better care of yourself. You have to take some vacation time."

"Max, I don't want to right now." He motioned toward the pile of folders in his basket. "I've got too much work to do."

"This isn't a suggestion, Brandon. I expect you to take some vacation time because you're too valuable to me and to your clients to lose." She stood. "You'd better start scheduling some time off because if you don't, next month, I will."

"But, Max…"

"Don't buck me on this, Brandon." She shook a finger at him. "If you don't schedule some time off, I'll clear your appointment calendar and lock you out of the office."

Brandon watched her leave the cubicle. He knew she was right. He was exhausted, physically, mentally and—he hated to admit it— spiritually. He put his elbows on the desk, dropped his head onto his hands, and tried to sort out his life.

Maybe he'd been doing this too long. Maybe the constant contact with parolees had made him jaded, cynical. Maxine had survived because she'd moved into administration, but that didn't appeal to him. He might as well work in a bank or a computer firm if he just wanted to sit in a chair and do paperwork.

No, he liked the contact with people. He'd been called to serve others. Was it possible this wasn't how he should serve anymore?

Before he decided that, he'd take a few days off, take a trip to visit friends. Rest and relax.

What he really wanted to do was spend that time with Francie. Not that she could take time off, but they could be together. Yes, a few days ago, he'd have said he'd spend those days off with Francie, but not now. She didn't want to see him again. He'd messed that up terribly.

What an idiot he'd been, when being with her was all he really wanted to do. Now that he was alone and unhappy, his concern about dating an ex-con didn't bother him anymore. He missed her terribly.

What was he going to do? He didn't know, but he knew one way to start.

"Dear Lord, I need your strength and guidance so much. Please remember me and lead me in your way. Please be with Francie." He paused to think of other words but realized those were sufficient for now. *"Amen."*

Chapter Twelve

The next week, Mike stopped by the diner again. As Francie finished waiting on the last customers, he asked, "So, how are things between you and Brandon?"

She didn't want to answer him, but she mumbled, "We aren't seeing each other anymore."

"What happened? I thought you were perfect for each other."

Julie brought Mike his order and sat down in the chair across the table. "The bum refused to introduce her to his family because she's an ex-con."

"Julie, don't—" Francie warned.

"What?" Mike's shout interrupted her words. He leaped to his feet and started toward Francie. "What happened?"

"Mike, please sit down," she told him. "I can't talk now. I need to serve my customers. I'll be back in a minute."

Unwillingly, he went back to the table but didn't touch the hamburger or fries.

When the last of the customers had left and Mike's food had grown cold, Francie sat down next to her cousin.

"Is what Julie said true? Did he break up with you because you're an ex-con?"

"No." Francie put her hand on his arm. "I broke up with him because he was ashamed of dating an ex-con. That was the problem. He couldn't get up the nerve to introduce me to his family."

"Did you tell him the truth?" Mike demanded.

"Mike," she said slowly and clearly. "He already knows the truth. I'm an ex-con. Nothing changes that."

"You didn't tell him everything, did you?" His voice was hard but his eyes flashed in anger. "You didn't tell him about me."

"Mike, I am an ex-con. Nothing," she repeated firmly, "*nothing* changes that."

"Then I'll tell him the truth." He pushed the chair back and stood.

"No, Mike." Francie grabbed his hand.

"Don't. Whatever you say won't change a thing. It will only make things worse. Please, just sit down and eat your hamburger. Don't mess in my life."

"It's my life, too, Francie."

She gripped his hand even harder when he tried to pull away from her. "Please, Mike, don't do anything. You want to be a doctor. Don't throw that away."

He didn't listen, just pulled himself from of her grasp and left.

"Francie, what's the matter?" Julie asked, putting her hands on Francie's shaking shoulders; this time, at last, Francie had broken down in tears.

"He's going to mess everything up," Francie sobbed. "His whole life." She slammed her hand down hard on the table. "And I can't do a thing about it."

That afternoon, Brandon looked at Mitzi Matthew's belligerent face again and stared down her threatening glare.

"I had to quit that job, Mr. Fairchild. I didn't like it. It didn't fit my talents and the boss didn't like me."

This was the fifth job she'd quit for those reasons.

When he looked away from Miss Matthews for a second, Brandon saw a young man nervously pacing in the reception area, glancing every now and then toward Brandon's cubicle. He thought it was Mike Fuller, but he looked different. Gone was the confident medical student he'd met. Now he looked young and scared. Why would Mike be here? He turned his attention back to his client.

"Mr. Warren has quite a good reputation, Miss Matthews. He's hired several ex-cons. They all say he's supportive and helpful."

"You're not calling me a liar, are you?" She attempted to threaten him with the hard glare that had probably scared a lot of people, but that didn't scare him.

No, right now he was aching for a fight. He'd welcome a chance to let loose the frustration and anger that gripped him when he thought about how badly he'd treated Francie. How could he have hurt the woman he loved so much? The answer was easy. He was a jerk.

So he was taking it out on Mitzi Matthews. Not at all professional to take his anger out on a parolee, but he didn't care. He answered Mitzi's glower with an even harder one of his own.

"I expect you to have a job," he said firmly.

Clearly Miss Matthews realized he wasn't bluffing. She stood as quickly as her enormous girth allowed and said, "I'll get another right away."

"And you'd better keep this one," he warned. "You know that working is a condition of your parole."

As he watched Miss Matthews stomp off fifteen minutes before the end of her appointment, the young man ran to Brandon's desk. "I'm Mike Fuller, Francie's cousin." He stuck his hand.

"Yes, I recognize you." Brandon stood and shook Mike's hand. "What can I do for you?"

"I need to talk to you." Mike looked around the area. "Privately."

"Why don't you sit down here?" Brandon motioned toward the chair Miss Matthews had vacated. "This is fairly private with the partitions and the noise from the reception area." Brandon settled back in his chair.

"It's about Francie." Mike sat and leaned forward, keeping his voice low and his eyes on Brandon's face.

"I can't talk about Miss Calhoun with you. What went on between us is personal, and what I know about her professionally is privileged." Brandon started to stand. "I don't want to talk about either of them."

"She didn't hold up that convenience store." The words rushed from Mike's mouth. When he finished, he looked at Brandon pleadingly before dropping his face in his hands and starting to cry.

Astonished, Brandon fell back in his chair and leaned toward Mike. "What do you mean? She confessed to robbing the store. According to the police report, she acted alone. She had the money, the ski mask and the jacket in the car with her. All the evidence pointed toward Francie."

"She was covering for me." Mike looked up, tears streaming down his cheeks.

Brandon put the box of tissues on his desk. "You're going to have to explain this better."

"Francie always wanted me to be a doctor. I made good grades and did really well in math and science. She encouraged me. Did everything she could to make that dream come true. Did too much." He wiped his eyes.

"You know about our family history?" Mike asked. "You know that my mother is in jail, as well as Francie's father and our uncle?"

Brandon nodded.

"You probably know Francie thinks we have a hereditary predilection toward being criminals." At Brandon's nod, he went on. "When I was eighteen, I felt that pull." He paused. "I'm really ashamed of this." He struggled to come up with words. "Francie was taking me out shopping. When we passed that convenience store, I told her I needed a loaf of bread. She parked the car while I went inside."

"*Francie* parked the car, and you went inside?" Brandon repeated.

"Yes, Francie had no idea what I was going to do. I put on a ski mask before I went in and threatened the clerk until he gave me the money in the cash register." Mike attempted to compose himself. "It was over a thousand dollars. I hadn't expected that much. I stuffed it in my jacket, ran outside and jumped into the car."

"Where Francie was waiting for you."

"Yes, where Francie was waiting for me. She saw the ski mask and knew what happened, of course. What reason to wear a ski mask in Texas other than to commit a robbery? Besides, I had money falling out of my pockets. She pulled the car around the corner, asked me for the money, made me take off my jacket and grabbed the ski mask." Mike blinked rapidly. "Then we heard sirens all around, so she pushed me out of the car and drove away."

"What did you do?"

"I felt so stupid. It hadn't been fun. The whole thing hadn't been exciting, like I thought it would, so I walked home and watched television."

"Then?"

"Weeks later, I found out Francie was in jail."

"And you didn't do anything about it?" Brandon was furious—at himself and at Mike. He should have followed his instinct from the first time he met Francie, the instinct that told him it was odd for a con artist to end up robbing a store. He should have had more faith in her.

"I didn't know what had happened. After she kicked me out of the car, Francie turned herself into the cops. I wasn't very tall then. We were about the same size and build. With the ski mask and jacket, Francie looked just like the pictures on the security camera. She and her court-appointed lawyer worked out a plea bargain. Francie told him to get her the best deal but quickly. She didn't want me to know what she was doing until it was too late."

"How did you find out that she took the fall for you? Why didn't you do anything then?"

"My foster mother told me after Francie was sentenced. That's the first time I even knew she'd been arrested. As soon as I found out, I visited her in lockup. That's when Francie said she taken the blame because didn't want one mistake to hurt my career. She said she had a bad record and her life wasn't going anywhere, but I had a future."

"And you allowed her to do that?"

Mike nodded and grabbed another handful of tissue to blow his nose. "I'm not proud of it. She sort of convinced me that I had to be a doctor. That's what she wanted." He looked up at Brandon with eyes overflowing with tears. "I keep telling myself I let her do it because I was a scared kid. I *was* really scared, but I should have done something."

"Why are you telling me now?"

"Because Francie said you were ashamed of her because she's an ex-con. I thought maybe if you knew that she shouldn't have been in prison, it might make a difference."

Brandon couldn't think of a thing to say, at least nothing that made him sound any better to Mike or to himself.

"And because I've been going to church

with her I realize I have to take responsibility for my life. I have to plead guilty to this crime and go to jail so her record can be expunged."

"Mike, no one is going to prosecute you for that crime, no one. They already solved it. Francie confessed and served time. That robbery was small potatoes as far as crime in Austin goes."

"But I'll confess." He pointed at himself. "I'll tell the truth. I'm the one who robbed the store."

"It's her confession against yours. Even if they did believe you—which, I promise you they won't because your cousin Francie is a very persuasive person and investigators will want to believe her—the county is not going to spend more time and money to convict another person and imprison him for the same offense."

"What am I going to do?" The rims of Mike's eyes were red against his pallor.

"You're going to take the gift your cousin gave you and become the best doctor you can. You are not going to repay her by breaking her heart and destroying her dream for you," Brandon said sternly.

"She spent time in prison for me."

"She loves you, Mike. She chose to do that."

"But now you're ashamed of her because she's an ex-con. She's not. She shouldn't be."

"Mike, that's not your problem. That's something Francie and I have to work out between us."

"Then you'll go talk to her?" Mike pleaded.

"Yes, but I don't know how much good it will do. I blew it, I really blew it. I have a feeling once your cousin makes up her mind, it's pretty hard to change."

"Yeah," Mike said. "Being stubborn is another family characteristic."

Brandon reached out his hand to shake Mike's. "Thanks for telling me. I'll try to do something about this."

But he had no idea what to do or where to start.

"This faith thing hasn't worked out as well as I'd hoped," Francie said to Julie as they cleaned up the tables after lunch. "It's not only what happened—or didn't happen—between Brandon and me. On top of that, there's school and work and my worry that Mike's going to do something dumb like confessing to the robbery. He'll end up in jail and who knows what Tim might do then?

"I thought faith would make my life better. I'd hoped the bad things would be easier to bear." Francie turned off the coffeepot and started to take it apart to clean. "Actually, I hoped bad things wouldn't happen to me anymore."

"I don't know what to say, Francie. I'm newer at this faith stuff than you, but I can see how you've changed. You were always a hard worker, determined to succeed, but since you've started going to church, I can see how much you've grown. You're much calmer and more patient than you were when we first met." Julie turned to watch Francie. "I know you've always cared about other people, but you were tough back then. You never communicated much, but you've talked Mike and me into going to church. Whether you see it or not, you're different, and you've changed Mike and me."

"Thank you, Julie, but if I'm changing, why do I feel this pressure? Why can't I share my burdens with God?"

"I think, maybe, that if this was easy, if faith meant there would be no problems, everyone would be a Christian. Why not? But faith means…" She stopped. "Francie, I don't know how to say what I mean, but look inside yourself."

* * *

That night, when Francie opened her Bible to read before going to bed, she found the verse, "Come to me all who are heavy-laden and I will give you peace."

She began to pray. *"Oh, God, where are you when I need you? Why doesn't loving you protect me from pain? Why does loving Brandon hurt so much? Please show me the way."*

As she dropped her head onto her hands, she started to think about what Julie had tried to explain, to remember what she had heard in sermons and Sunday-school class, what she had read.

When she looked inside herself, a deep peace filled her.

All of the bad things would have happened even if she hadn't turned to the Lord. Faith didn't mean nothing bad would happen. It meant she wouldn't be alone during the hard time. She leaned back and wiped her eyes.

"Dear God," she prayed. *"You're always with me. I'm the one who moved away. Even when life is hard, I know you're with me. Time after time, you give me strength to make it through. Thank you."*

When Francie left the diner the next afternoon, Brandon was standing outside the door.

She tried to turn around and walk in the other direction, but the urgency in his voice stopped her.

"Francie, just a minute, please. Could we talk for a minute? Maybe at that little park?"

She didn't want to, not at all, but shouldn't she? Didn't she really have to? It was that kindness and gentleness business again.

She walked around him and headed the short distance to the park. Once there, she stood and waited for Brandon to speak, showing, she felt, great self-control because listening to him was not at all what she wanted to do. The tapping of her foot contradicted her efforts to be patient.

"I'm sorry, Francie."

"Thank you. I forgive you." At least she was trying to. She nodded and started toward the street.

"Would you sit down for a minute?" His voice rose. She could see the effort it took for him to calm himself before he continued. He said in a more controlled voice, "This is going to be easier if I don't think you're going to walk away while I'm trying to explain."

She didn't care one bit if it was easier for him but realized she had a really bad attitude, the old Francie's attitude. Struggling to remind herself of the Francie she wanted to be, she settled on the bench farthest from him. When he sat next to her, she moved to the very end, keeping her hands behind her when he reached out to take one of them.

"Mike came to talk to me."

She bit her lip. "I was afraid he would."

"I was very impressed with him. He took responsibility for his actions and wants to make amends. He wanted to confess to the crime and go to prison. He wants you to be cleared."

"You know I wouldn't allow that to happen. I hope you talked him out of that."

"Yes, I told him it was doubtful he'd be prosecuted and, if he pursued it, that would ruin your dream."

"Thank you." Francie stood again.

"Would you sit down?" Brandon asked, his voice laced with frustration. The emotion in his voice caused her to turn and study him.

"I'm sorry," he said. "But there's something I really need to say, and you keep trying to leave."

He looked very unlike his usual well-dressed self. His tie hung loosely around his neck and his hair was rumpled from running his hands through it.

"Go on." She considered moving to another bench but Brandon would probably follow her. She resumed her place on the bench, as far away from him as possible.

Before Brandon could say anything, the man with the black dog started into the park. He looked up at Brandon, turned when he saw Brandon's scowl and hurried out to the street.

Brandon turned his attention back to Francie. "You did a courageous and loving thing, Francie, when you took the punishment for him."

"Anyone would have done that."

"No, anyone wouldn't. Most people who are prosecuted claim they're innocent, over and over. No one serves time to protect someone else. You're a remarkable woman." He tried to take her hand again, but she refused to allow it, again.

"Thank you."

"I didn't tell the complete truth the other day."

"Oh?" She studied Brandon for a moment.

He looked uncomfortable. He tugged his tie off and stuffed it in a pocket before saying, "I love you, Francie."

The statement shocked her. For a moment she had no idea what to say. Finally she realized it was much too late for the words to make any difference, even those words she'd longed to hear him say. What did he expect her to do? Fall into his arms?

She said, "Thank you," very politely.

"Would you stop—" Brandon stopped his words "Francie, I'm trying to communicate with you. Won't you please talk to me?"

"I don't know that we have much to talk about, Brandon. No matter what you or Mike says, I'm still an ex-con."

"But you didn't do the crime, Francie."

"That doesn't change the fact that I did do the time. That doesn't change the fact that I was convicted twice of other crimes. My father's in prison. So are my aunt and uncle, and you just found out my nephew held up a convenience store. We are not a model family. I'm the same person you were ashamed of before."

"But, Francie—"

"Brandon, have you told your parents about me yet?"

"No, I haven't had time."

"You've had plenty of time. We ended our relationship two weeks ago. Or, you could have told them about me after you talked to Mike. Either way, you've decided not to, and that says more about your feelings than any words. You're still ashamed of me." She waited.

"I'm not, not really."

Not much of an answer. "Why haven't you told your parents?"

When he didn't answer, she said, "I guess that tells me everything."

She stood and started away before turning back to ask, "You won't tell anyone what Mike said, will you?"

"No."

"Thank you." She started to leave again.

"Francie, I love you." He stood and moved to stand in front of her.

"That's an odd kind of love, Brandon." She spoke clearly and purposefully. "Love isn't something you hide so you won't be embarrassed."

"Maybe God planned it this way, Francie. Did you ever think of that? Maybe God wanted us to meet, but the only people I ever meet are my parolees."

"Certainly God could have figured out a much better idea, one that didn't involve having me spend time in prison. Maybe we could have run into each other on the street."

"Francie?" he asked when she didn't say

anything. "Isn't there anything I can say to change things? To make you forgive me?"

"Brandon, one of the most important things I've learned over the past few months is that I am a child of God. I'm learning to respect myself, and I refuse to be around a person who doesn't respect me, who can't accept me as the person I am."

"I'm trying, Francie. This is new to me, too. I've never been in love before."

"I don't think you are now."

"Francie..."

"Brandon, I don't think I could ever believe you again. I thought you cared about me. I had so much confidence in you. I even thought you were better than I am."

"Why would you think that?"

"Because I was blinded by you, I guess. Amazed that a man like you would want to be with me."

"Why wouldn't I?"

"Brandon, you answered that question yourself when you decided not to take me to meet your family."

"I was wrong."

She shrugged. "You knew from the beginning our relationship wouldn't lead any place because you couldn't get over my past, and yet you allowed me to fall in love with you. I'm not sure I can forgive that." She paused and closed her eyes for a moment. "But I'm going to have to, Brandon."

Then she walked out of the park and toward the street.

He didn't try to stop her.

"Manny, I saw Brandon out there." Julie stood at the counter between the kitchen and the diner watching the cook chop vegetables. "When Francie left, he was waiting for her. I wonder what he wants."

"Francie will take care of it." He diced another carrot for the vegetable soup.

"I know, but she's such a great person. I hate for her to suffer." Julie moved back toward the tables to start putting the chairs up.

"You're a fine one to talk," he said.

Julie whirled to look at Manny who was still slicing vegetables and didn't meet her eyes. "What?"

"Nothing." He continued to slice potatoes.

"You said, 'You're a fine one to talk.'"

"If you heard me, why did you ask me to repeat it?" He concentrated very hard on making straight cuts in the slice of potato.

"Manny, I know what you said, but I have

no idea what you mean." She reached out over the counter to put her hand on his arm. "Please talk to me, Manny."

He looked up at her. "Julie, I've been in love with you since I started working here. How long has that been? Five years? I thought we were going to get married, but first you break the engagement. Then you treat me like a jerk. Now you want to be friends." He shook a potato at her. "Do you know how much that hurt me? Julie, I want to be more than friends."

"What?" Julie dropped into a chair.

"I said—"

"You love me? You still love me?"

"Said so, didn't I?"

"But you were the one who didn't want to get married unless I signed the diner over to you." She pointed at him, confused but hopeful.

"Julie, I'm the man in our relationship. Back then, I thought the man should own the diner. That's the way I was brought up."

"When you said that, I didn't know if you loved me or if you wanted the diner." She bit her lip. "That really hurt, Manny."

"I don't want you to sign the diner over

to me anymore. Does that help make up your mind?"

"Manny, why don't you come out here and talk to me?"

"I'm more comfortable slicing vegetables."

Julie stood and walked into the kitchen. "Does this mean we're engaged again?"

Manny shook his head. "I didn't like being engaged. Let's go ahead and get married."

"I'd like that." She picked up an onion and began to slice it.

"Don't think this means I'll do whatever you want. Doesn't mean I'll go to church with you."

She didn't say a word, just sliced another onion and smiled at Manny. "We'll see about that," she whispered.

This time when Julie slid into the booth, she was wearing such a big smile Francie couldn't help but return it.

"What happened?" Francie closed her book and leaned toward her boss.

"Manny and I," Julie hesitated. "We're getting married."

"What? You're getting married? When did this happen?"

"Yesterday after lunch we got to talking,

and he still loves me, and I...well, I never got over the man."

"You're getting married." Francie took Julie's hand. "I am so happy for you."

And she was. She really was.

When Francie left the diner on Thursday afternoon, Mike was waiting for her. There always seemed to be someone waiting for her. Communication would probably be easier if she had a phone.

"Did Brandon tell you that I went to see him?" her cousin asked as soon as he saw her.

"Yes." She moved closer and glared up at him. "Why'd you do such a dumb thing?"

"It wasn't dumb, Francie. I never should have let you take responsibility for my crime."

"Don't tell me that, Mike. I chose to do it. You couldn't do anything about it until it was too late. And it's still too late to change what happened."

"I should have done something. I should have known what you'd do when you took the mask and jacket and kicked me out of the car."

"Well, you didn't, and that's okay with me." Her expression softened. "Mike, you were just a kid. I didn't want you to have a criminal record. I didn't want you to go through what I did. I wanted you to have a future. Besides, it wasn't all that big a deal."

"Tim tells me it was a big deal. He said they used to beat you up in prison and there wasn't a thing you could do about it." He paused.

"Oh, I just told Tim that to scare him, to get him to give me the gun."

Mike shook his head, "I don't believe that. I think it was that bad for you."

"Mike, accept what happened and go on with your life. I have. There's nothing you can change now. All I ask is that you have a good life. Marry Cynthia, have kids, give me more little cousins and be happy."

"What can I do, Francie? What can I do to thank you? To make up for everything?"

"Nothing. Just being able to live your life, that's all I'll ever want." She stopped. "Well, there is one more thing. Is your car running or are you tinkering with it?"

"It's going fine. Why?"

"I need to go to Gatesville Saturday to see my father. Can you drive me?"

Chapter Thirteen

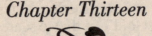

"Thanks for coming again," Sam Calhoun said. "It's good to see you."

Francie smiled at her father through the window between them. "How're are things going with you, Dad?"

"You know how prison is, Francie. The same day after day."

Francie could think of nothing to say and her father seemed to be struggling with something. As the silence stretched between then, he changed position in the chair and studied his hands.

Finally he looked up at Francie. "This is hard for me to say, Angel, but after all these years, I have to."

"What is it Dad?"

"I've thought about this a lot since your last visit."

When he dropped his eyes again, she said, "You're scaring me. What's the matter?"

This time when he looked up, his face serious. "I want to apologize, Francie. I know you have trouble trusting others. A lot of that's my fault and I'm sorry."

"Thanks, Dad, but you don't have to say that. I've made more than my share of bad choices on my own."

"Francie, you blame yourself for everything. You shouldn't. Everyone you ever cared about ran out on you. That can't make you feel secure."

"I don't—"

"But none of that's your fault," he went on. "Lots of the blame belongs to your mother, but it's mostly my fault, Angel. I'm your father, and I should have been a better one. I can't apologize for Maisy, but I'm sorry for how much I hurt you." He bowed his head again.

Francie didn't know what to say. For almost a minute, she studied his graying hair and the small bald spot as her father kept his face in his hands and struggled for control.

"Being a parent is hard. You probably tried your best," she said.

That brought his head up and she could see tears in his eyes. Tough Sam Calhoun had tears in his eyes.

"No, I didn't. When we didn't have enough money, I gave up. I held up that liquor store. I didn't have a lot of options, but I had some. I could've gotten a job like everyone else's father, but that was too much trouble, too much responsibility. I've always been short on that.

"And none of the jobs I could get paid enough for everything I wanted." He shook his head. "I could've told you I didn't have the money, and we were going to have to cut back. I could've told you that I couldn't afford to take you to the movies, but that I loved you, even if I couldn't buy you stuff."

She would've been okay with that.

"You were a great kid. You would have understood. There were plenty of things I could have done, but I chose armed robbery instead."

"What's the use in talking about this now?" She shifted in the hard plastic chair. "It doesn't change anything. Besides, I'm past that." She was getting a little uncomfortable emotionally, too. This seemed like more sharing than she was ready for. "It's okay, Dad."

"No, it isn't. I'll never forget how you looked that day the cops arrested me at home.

What a terrible thing to see your father led out in handcuffs."

She'd never forgotten that, either. She'd cried until her mother had slapped her and told her to shut up.

"Francie, your mother wasn't any great shakes, either, not as a wife and certainly not as a mother. After all, she chose to abandon a child." His took out a handkerchief and blew his nose. "Do you remember her at all?"

"Not very well." She recalled a tall woman with bright blond hair who always scowled at her and had a heavy hand. "She was always disappointed in me."

"Not in you. Probably in me. Maisy and I probably never should have gotten married. We should never have had a child. But I'm glad we did. As little as I've seen you, you've brought me a lot of happiness, except when you were in jail. Of course, that wasn't unexpected with me as an example. I'm sorry I didn't do better."

"Thanks, Dad, for what you've said." She considered his words for almost a minute. "I don't know exactly what to say, but I'm going to think about it, pray about it."

"Francie, you should be proud of yourself, too. Look what you're doing with your life.

You got your GED. Your mother and I didn't finish high school. You're going to college and working. You have to be proud of yourself, not ashamed. You're a *good* example for the entire family. I don't know where you got the strength and gumption to change."

He put his hand on the glass and she pressed hers against it. "I'll be getting out in a few years, Francie."

"Are you going straight then?"

"I'm going to have to. I don't want to die in here. I'm too old to run from the cops any more. They're getting younger and faster, from what the new guys tell me. You're going to have to help me, show me how you changed your life."

"I'll be glad to, Dad. I'm sure we can find you a job. I'll even take you to church."

"I'll accept the help on the job, Angel, but not church. Don't think that's going to help. There's no way an old sinner like me can change that much, but can you forgive me for what I've done in the past?"

"Of course I forgive you, Dad."

"Thanks, Francie.

They talked for a few more minutes before her father said, "Your cousin Mike wrote me. He told me about you and this Brandon fellow. Said you broke up with this guy. Mike said the man was ashamed of you because of your record."

"Dad, I don't want to talk about this." She searched for another topic of conversation. "What do you think about the Cowboys? Do you think… "

"Mike wrote you wouldn't want to talk about it, but he thinks it's important. I do, too."

"Dad, we've never talked about anything, at least nothing important. Why start now?"

"It's about time we started. Francie, I'm not getting any younger. I'd like to try to be a real father to you before I die."

"Are you sick?" Francie asked.

"No, but I'm getting old, Francie. Prison ages people fast. And I've missed out on a lot, knowing you, having a real family. Oh, sure, that's my fault, but just this once, Francie, would you talk to me? Make me feel like there's something between us?"

Francie had barely accepted the fact he was her father. She'd thought their relationship would build slowly. Right now, she didn't want to listen to his advice. With a deep breath, she reminded herself of the fruit of the spirit before she spoke.

"There's no reason to talk about Brandon.

We dated for a while, but now it's over. I'm going on with my life." She pushed her chair back as if she would to leave if he didn't drop it.

"Angel, I've been a miserable failure as a father. It would mean a lot to me if we could start over. If I could help you for once, maybe just listen."

She couldn't dispute that. He hadn't been the best father. He hadn't been a particularly bad father because he'd seldom been around, but he was the only one she had. So she pulled the chair forward a little. "I don't think you can help me. This is a big mess."

"Wouldn't forgiving him help?"

"That's not fair, Dad. We were talking about forgiving you, not him."

"I did far worse to you than Brandon ever did. I let all these years go by before I asked your forgiveness, probably made you accept blame for stuff you weren't responsible for. If you can forgive me, why not him?"

"It's different, Dad."

"Has he asked forgiveness yet?"

She nodded.

"If you can forgive me, why can't you forgive him?" he repeated.

"It's not the same." She met his eyes. "He

really hurt me. I don't know if I can ever believe in him."

"I'm not asking for that. You don't even have to see him again, but can't you forgive the man? Isn't that what you Christians are supposed to do?"

She nodded again. "But I don't want to. I know I should, but—"

"Angel, if I've learned anything in my life, it's that carrying around anger really messes you up. Look at your mother. She was always angry that I couldn't find a job. Look at me. I was always angry because she kept complaining, all the time. Look what happened to us. You don't want to end up bitter and alone."

Francie started to answer but the guard interrupted to take her father back to his cell.

"Goodbye, Francie. Thanks for forgiving me. And that Brandon fellow, don't give up on him. Try to forgive him, too. We all need help at some time."

On the ride back to Austin, Francie asked Mike about his plans, about Cynthia, before finally asking, "Mike, do you really want to be a doctor or did I push you into it?"

"At first, I didn't. I took those courses because I wanted to please you, Francie. I owe you so much."

"Mike, I never wanted you to become a doctor because *I* wanted that for you. Don't spend the rest of your life paying me back."

"I'm not, Francie. Besides, now I want to be a doctor. When I started taking the pre-med classes, I found out that was exactly what I wanted to be." He took her hand. "Thanks for shoving me—hard—in that direction."

After a little more conversation, Francie leaned back and pretended to sleep as she pondered what her father had said. She was finally mature and confident enough to understand that for all these years she'd taken responsibility for actions that had never been her fault— or mostly hadn't been her fault. She felt a great lightening of spirit with that burden gone.

Could she forgive her parents? Well, as a Christian— she had no choice. Like her, they were flawed people. They'd messed her life up, but they'd messed up their own pretty well even before she'd been born. In addition, there was no reason not to. Her father was a broken man with no past and little future. Her mother—how could she hold a grudge against a woman she hadn't seen in almost twenty years? A woman who had abandoned her own child was too pitiful and weak to waste time hating. Besides, all that happened so many long ago. The pain had faded years earlier. Now it was time to let go of the anger.

What about Brandon? Could she excuse what he'd done, how he'd treated her? As her father said, that's what Christians did, and she knew that. She hadn't changed much if she refused to forgive him, had she?

No matter how she tried to think of reasons not to forgive Brandon, she had to turn each down. No matter how she tried to justify her inflexible stance, she couldn't, but she wasn't able to forgive him yet.

The next day in church, she finally gave up her rationalization as the congregation said the Lord's Prayer.

"Forgive us our sins as we forgive those who sin against us," she prayed with the joined voices.

How could she sit in church and pray those words, how could she expect God to forgive her for the terrible things she'd done in the past and the mistakes she'd probably continue to make—how could she expect God to forgive her for anything if she refused to forgive Brandon?

She couldn't.

Released from the weight of that choice, she spent the rest of Sunday studying and planning how to talk to Brandon. No matter how uncomfortable seeing him again would be, she had to do it.

After she finished serving breakfast Monday morning, Francie called the parole office from the diner and left a message with the receptionist. Only a few minutes later, the phone rang.

"Hello?" she answered.

"Francie? Did you call?"

Brandon's voice sounded a little uncertain, but so wonderful, so dear.

"What did you want?" he asked. "Are you all right?"

"I need to talk to you. Can you meet me this afternoon?"

"I'll take the entire day off if you want me to, Francie. And tomorrow. I'll meet you any time, any place."

"None of that's necessary. What about two o'clock this afternoon? This will only take a minute."

"At the park?"

No, she didn't want to go there. It held

both good and bad memories, but the bad ones still hurt. "Why don't you come here?"

"To the diner? With Manny and Julie listening?"

Yes, knowing her friends were close would make her feel stronger and more confident. "I'll tell them to leave us alone."

"Good luck with that, but I'll do whatever you want. Two o'clock at the diner."

When he came in ten minutes early, Francie had to close her eyes for a second. She wondered how she could do this, how she could talk to him again without wanting to hold his hand or bursting into tears or doing something horribly emotional which would embarrass her greatly. All of those would be terrible mistakes with the wide chasm separating them.

"Dear Lord, please give me strength and the right words to use," she whispered before she walked toward him.

"Why don't you sit in that booth in the corner." She pointed. "I'll get you a piece of pie and some coffee."

"No thanks, Francie. I don't need anything, except to talk to you, to be with you." He motioned her to precede him and followed her to the booth. When she sat down, he slid in next to her.

She hadn't expected that. When she'd thought this meeting out, he'd been farther away, opposite her. In her plans, she'd been rational and logical and under control. Sitting next to him blew that strategy out of the water.

"Why don't you move over there?" She pointed across the table.

"I like it here." He turned sideways, put his elbow on the table and leaned his cheek against his fist, watching her. "I've missed you."

He was not making this easy.

"I want to tell you that I forgive you."

There. That was it. That was all she'd planned to say. If he wasn't blocking her in, she'd get up and walk away.

"You said that before."

"I didn't mean it then," she confessed. "That was wrong of me. I mean it now."

She looked at him but he didn't move. "That's all. You can go now." She smiled in an effort to soften the words but failed. They hadn't sounded kind and most certainly weren't courteous.

He didn't say anything, just looked at her for almost a minute. "I was really glad when you called this morning," he said. "If you hadn't, I would have called you."

"Why?" This was not going at all as she'd expected.

"I wanted to see you. I hoped you'd calmed down and we could talk."

"We just talked. I said I forgive you. That's all." She glanced up, hoping that Manny or Julie would come save her, but she couldn't even see them. Why weren't they standing in the kitchen watching or puttering around in the diner?

"Goodbye." She tried to gently nudge him out of the booth with her elbow. He didn't move. Short of planting her back against the wall and pushing him with both feet, nothing would move him. With a sigh, she gave up.

"Francie, I love you, and I'm not going to let you get away, no matter what you do or say."

"You can't love me. You're ashamed of me."

"No, that's not true." He met her eyes. His voice became serious. "I'm ashamed of myself. You're the best person I've ever met, and I was so full of who I was and my family, I couldn't see that. I can't tell you how sorry I am. I was a condescending, conceited jerk who couldn't trust you, who couldn't see how you've changed, who couldn't accept you as the remarkable person you are. Please, Francie, please forgive me for that."

"I just did." My, condescending and conceited he'd called himself. He must really be sorry about this.

"But you haven't forgotten what I did."

"Brandon, have you prayed about this? Did you ask God to forgive you?"

"I've been praying constantly since the second time you told me to get out of your life."

He took her hand. That was not at all fair.

"Francie, God forgave me, I'm sure. God knows how sorry I am, how willing I am to try to make this up to you."

"Good." She shoved him a little, trying to make him move, but he didn't. Then she attempted to pull her hand from his, but he didn't let go.

As if he didn't notice her efforts, he continued, "But I need you to forgive me, too. If you don't, I don't know what I'm going to do. Please, Francie, I need you to do that."

"I said I did." With him holding her hand and sitting so close, her voice cracked a little.

"Then I'll pick you up for dinner."

She searched for another argument. "I can't go to dinner with someone who's ashamed of me."

He shook his head and smiled. "I'm not ashamed of you. Not one bit."

"I think you are." Why was he feeling so confident when she felt like she was sinking? "Oh, why?"

"You never take me anywhere your friends or family go. You never told your parents about me."

"For the first part, I plan to. On the second, you're wrong." He grinned at her. "I told my family all about you the same day you told me to get lost—the second time."

"You told them about me?" Her eyes zoomed up to his face. "Did you tell them I'm an ex-con?"

"I did. They were furious."

"I imagine they were." She bit her lip. "Of course they would be. No parents could be happy to know their son was dating an ex-con."

"They're not mad because you're an ex-con. They're furious with *me.* They couldn't understand why I didn't trust them enough to know they'd welcome anyone I love."

"What?" She blinked.

"And my sisters hit me. Hard. Can you see the bruises? He pointed to his cheek.

"They what?" She inspected his face but saw no sign of injury.

"Well, maybe they just beat me up metaphorically, which doesn't leave a lot of bruises, but they do want to know when they get to meet you. They can't believe their old bachelor brother fell in love and kept it—and you—from them."

"Brandon, I'm an ex-con."

"They'll all love you."

"Brandon, I'm an ex-con," she repeated slowly and clearly in case he'd forgotten or didn't understand her.

"Francie, that doesn't bother me, and it doesn't bother my family at all. Don't let my stupidity keep us apart. I really love you. I know I was wrong. I hate it that I hurt you so much. I'm having trouble forgiving myself for what I did."

"Brandon." She searched for words. He seemed to have answered every one of her objections and worries, except one. "How can I ever trust you again?" She blinked to keep tears from spilling onto her cheeks.

"I don't know." He kept his gaze steady on her face. "Just give me a chance. Please give us a chance." He reached out to blot a tear with his thumb, then caressed her cheek. "Please, Francie, give me a chance, give me time to prove that you can."

"I don't know." But she was beginning to believe she could.

"I'm begging you to, Francie, because I think we have a wonderful future ahead. I see you and me and a dozen little girls with big blue eyes and curly black hair."

"A dozen?" She allowed the concept to sink in. "Our daughters?"

"Maybe not that many, but I want to create a family with you, Francie, I want to sit in church with you, sharing our faith with our children. I want to spend the rest of my life with you, Francie."

"I'm still not sure, Brandon." But she was getting closer to believing. As much as she struggled not to give in, not to think this could happen, she was beginning to believe him.

"All right. Let's try one more thing." He pulled out his cell phone and dialed. "Mom?" he said. "I'd like to bring Francie home for dinner tonight. Is that all right?" He listened. "No, don't invited Susanne and Miriam. I'd like it to be just the four of us." He nodded. "Okay. See you at seven." Then he flipped the phone shut and put it in his pocket.

"Now do you believe me?"

She nodded. "But I can't go. I don't have anything to wear."

"They don't care what you wear, Francie. Jeans, your blue blouse, your yellow uniform, it doesn't matter. They'll love you as much as I do. Well, maybe almost as much as I do."

"But you have a big house, right?"

"My parents have a big house. I have a much smaller apartment. What difference does that make?"

"If you don't know how much difference that makes…"

"If this bothers you, we'll go out to eat, to the place we went before."

"Brandon, you have to understand. I don't have anything to wear to meet your family, not at a restaurant, not in a mansion."

"It's not a mansion, Francie, just a nice house." He studied her face. "That's not the real reason, is it?"

She shook her head. "Brandon, I'm so different. You know that. You've said that. How could I ever fit in with your family? They're so different. We're so different." She shook her head.

"If I can accept your family, I don't understand why you can't accept mine."

Her gaze leaped to his face. She was amazed to realize that was exactly what she was doing, not accepting who he was or his family.

"Francie, my family and the fact that I have a little money are as much a part of me as your past is of you. I hope you can accept that."

She considered that. "Yes, I can, but Brandon—" She closed her eyes, trying to explain how frightened she was. "I'm still struggling to find my place in the world I know. I'm afraid to leave it. I don't think I can do this," she whispered.

"Francie, look at me."

She did, amazed at the love she saw in his eyes.

"You can do this," he said. "Together, we can do this. With God's help and blessing, we can do this."

Maybe they could. If she wanted to be with him, she would have to try.

And she really wanted to be with him.

"You are filled with love, joy and peace. Everyone will see that," he said. "You are very beautiful."

He kissed her, lovingly and gently. With that kiss, she knew he truly thought she was beautiful.

As they kissed, Francie heard cheering from the kitchen.

"Let's get out of here," she said.

"Let's go to that little park."

She nodded and took his hand as he slid out of the booth.

"That man and his little black dog better not be there because I want to kiss you and show you how much I love you," he glanced at the kitchen, "in privacy."

Epilogue

Francie looked down the pew. Next to her sat Brandon. On the other side were Mike, Cynthia and Tim. Mike had told her he and Cynthia were going to get married when she finished her degree. As for Tim, well, she didn't know what would happen with Tim. He was still troubled but he was making good grades and coming to church with his brother.

As she watched, Julie slipped into the pew. Maybe Manny would join his wife some day.

Joy filled Francie as she looked at those she loved. She glanced down at her hand to touch her new ring: gold with a beautiful emerald. In two months, another ring would join that one. In a year or two, she hoped they would have a baby to dedicate here.

"Dear God," she whispered, *"thank you for guiding me to your church. Everything I have comes from the path you started me on that evening, from the joyful spirit you blessed me with."*

Then she took Bandon's hand and turned her thoughts to the service.

＊＊＊＊＊

Dear Reader,

Because I've been active in the church since my parents first enrolled me in the church nursery, I've wanted to write an inspirational novel. The problem was, I could never think of an idea until Francie Calhoun, her larcenous family and her conversion suddenly appeared. How Francie uses her gifts to find a sustaining faith, which changes her life and the lives of her friends, is the theme of this novel. That she also finds love is an additional joy.

One of my favorite Scriptures is the list of the fruits of the spirit in Galatians, so it made sense to use them as Francie learns to live her life as a Christian.

I have to confess that I am not a patient person, but writing this book has changed me—or, at least, *begun* to change me. I don't like sitting in traffic, but now when I have to wait, I remind myself that patience is a fruit of the spirit. This has helped me learn to sit in traffic jams almost an hour-long and think of something else, like the plot of my next novel—at least, most of the time.

I am blessed to be able to share my faith with you in this novel. I hope the story of Francie and her growth will bring blessings to your life.

Jane Myers Perrine

And now, turn the page
for a sneak preview of
SUSPICION OF GUILT,
the second book in
THE MAHONEY SISTERS *miniseries*
by Tracey V. Bateman,
part of Steeple Hill's exciting new line,
Love Inspired Suspense!
On Sale in September 2005
from Steeple Hill Books.

Prologue

The night swirled around her. Black, stabbing darkness conjuring terrible shadows from childhood nightmares. Leaves hovered like a vampire's cape, suffocating. Fear gripped her. Branches tossed in the breeze—razor-sharp fingers ready to slice her to shreds.

Hurry! Hurry! Hurry!

A low half growl, half whine came from the Doberman behind the fence next door. She jerked her head at the sound, heart pounding in her ears like the thrum of a thousand drums.

Shh. "It's okay," she whispered. Don't give me away. I'm so close to accomplishing my goal. The dog sat—watching but silent.

Relief flooded her as she turned back to her

task. Denni Mahoney, with all of her sweet-ness and niceness…

Shards of rage pierced through her heart at the thought of Denni getting what she wanted. She didn't deserve it. A mastermind of deception. Denni had fooled them all.

Everyone but me. The thought made her smile with grim determination.

With a shaky hand she reached for the out-side faucet. Hesitated. One twist and the bro-ken pipe would send water rushing inside the house instead of flowing to the ground. The basement would flood.

She grasped the faucet tight and gave it a quick turn.

Water spewed.

The Doberman barked.

Her heart rate escalated. She pushed to her feet, gulping down the fear. She crept across the yard. Relief gradually shoved away the terror of night as she found safety.

Chapter One

Shock, disbelief, horror…all vied for first place in Denni Mahoney's chest as she stared at the foot of water standing in her basement. Water. Just standing there where water was never meant to be. Despair clutched her heart and squeezed the breath from her lungs. She shook her head, pressing her palm to her forehead.

What next?

"We'll get to the bottom of this." Behind her, Detective Reece Corrigan's tone was hard-edged, resolute, but the warmth of his hand on her shoulder evoked a strange sense of comfort.

"You have to admit it definitely could be one of them. Why do you insist that all five of the girls are innocent?"

The warm, comforting fuzzies turned to cold stone. She didn't have to admit any such thing and she was sick of his suspicions being centered on the girls. Anger shoved down the tears clogging her throat, and she shook off his hand.

Standing on the fourth step from the bottom of the basement stairs, Denni watched a hardback book float across the water covering the concrete floor. *A Tale of Two Cities.* A birthday gift from her mom when she'd turned fifteen. Little by little her memories of Mom were being destroyed. It had been ten years since her death, and only photos provided a clear picture of her face anymore.

Denni grimaced and abruptly turned away, but Reece's body on the step above her blocked her flight up. Even when she sent him her fiercest frown, he didn't budge.

She drew in the subtle scent of his spicy aftershave. Understated appeal. She liked that about him. The guy had to know how he affected women—a muscular physique and a masculinity that intimidated Denni, yet left her wishing he'd stay close.

"Well?" he asked, the tension in his voice replaced by a subtle, low tone that seeped over her like a gentle rain.

She gaped, fighting the warmth creeping to her cheeks. "Well what?" she whispered.

"I'm going to have to question them again. Who should I speak with first this time?"

"Oh, Reece," she said, hearing the fatigue in her tone. She was so tired. So very, very tired. "Leave the girls alone, will you? How can you blame them for a flood?"

Her girls. Troubled, ex-foster-care kids who were too old to stay in the system but too young to be out on their own. As a social worker, she had grown tired of seeing so many of these girls end up on public assistance, their own children placed in foster care, so she'd opened a home.

Only five young women lived with her, but if her experiment panned out, she had commitments from several local churches to help buy two more homes, each housing ten girls. Monday she was supposed to host a luncheon for the liaisons from each of these churches. How could she explain to potential sponsors that the cops suspected her girls of sabotage?

Denni glanced back at the basement, searching for escape from the confrontation that was surely to come. It was either hike down the steps and swim through the murky water or face Reece's rock-solid stubbornness. She sighed, knowing there was only one logical choice. She'd have to face him.

Forcing herself away from the sight of so many of her treasures soaked and more than likely ruined, she braced for the coming conflict, a tiresome, constant echo of accusation.

"Admit it," he demanded.

Deliberately, she lifted her gaze and met his. His steely green eyes silently commanded her to accept the possibility.

"I admit only one thing. It looks as though someone is trying to sabotage my efforts to make a nice home for these girls." A sigh pushed from her lungs. "What I can't figure out is why."

Detective Corrigan scowled. "That's what I'm here for, and I have to tell you…"

Denni raised her hand to stop his opinion from flying out of his mouth. "What possible motive could any of them have to sabotage their own home? Where would they go?"

Leaving him to mull over that bit of reason, she scraped against his bomber jacket as she maneuvered around him and marched to the top of the stairs. He followed her into the kitchen.

"That's the one thing I can't put my finger on. It doesn't make a lot of sense, but maybe the person we're dealing with here doesn't think along rational lines."

"All my girls are rational," Denni snapped.

His amusement was more than apparent in the upward curve of his lips. "Then I guess they must take after you," he drawled.

ileged." Brandon started to stand. "I don't want to talk about either of them."

"She didn't hold up that convenience store." The words rushed from Mike's mouth. When he finished, he looked at Brandon pleadingly before dropping his face in his hands and starting to cry.

Astonished, Brandon fell back in his chair and leaned toward Mike. "What do you mean? She confessed to robbing the store. According to the police report, she acted alone. She had the money, the ski mask and the jacket in the car with her. All the evidence pointed toward Francie."

"She was covering for me." Mike looked up, tears streaming down his cheeks.

Brandon put the box of tissues on his desk. "You're going to have to explain this better."

"Francie always wanted me to be a doctor. I made good grades and did really well in math and science. She encouraged me. Did everything she could to make that dream come true. Did too much." He wiped his eyes. "You know about our family history?" Mike asked. "You know that my mother is in jail, as well as Francie's father and our uncle?"

Brandon nodded.

"You probably know Francie thinks we have a hereditary predilection toward being criminals." At Brandon's nod, he went on. "When I was eighteen, I felt that pull." He paused. "I'm really ashamed of this." He struggled to come up with words. "Francie was taking me out shopping. When we passed that convenience store, I told her I needed a loaf of bread. She parked the car while I went inside."

"*Francie* parked the car, and you went inside?" Brandon repeated.

"Yes, Francie had no idea what I was going to do. I put on a ski mask before I went in and threatened the clerk until he gave me the money in the cash register." Mike attempted to compose himself. "It was over a thousand dollars. I hadn't expected that much. I stuffed it in my jacket, ran outside and jumped into the car."

"Where Francie was waiting for you."

"Yes, where Francie was waiting for me. She saw the ski mask and knew what happened, of course. What reason to wear a ski mask in Texas other than to commit a robbery? Besides, I had money falling out of my pockets. She pulled the car around the corner, asked me for the money, made me take off my